Praise For Clarissa

"Speculative science-fiction that really does veer off into worlds, scenarios and experiences previously unknown. The melding of genres, then pushing the boundaries to see where it takes both the readers and the author – trademark Drinkwater."
Cheryl M-M's Book Blog

"The world building is fantastic. An action packed read that keeps you on the edge of your seat."
Splashesintobooks

"From the moment the alarm sounds I was tense and on edge. What follows left me in awe of Karl Drinkwater's creativity."
Jera's Jamboree

"What an enjoyable ride this book was! Action, mystery and a sassy main character which is everything I want in a sci-fi story."
On The Shelf Reviews

"Clarissa explores themes of otherness in a number of ways. A little girl in a world of adults. A person of color in a very white society. A prodigy with poor social skills. An alien species making contact. Drinkwater reminds us that otherness brings both dangers and opportunities."
Scintilla

CLARISSA

LOST TALES OF SOLACE BOOK 3

KARL DRINKWATER

ORGANIC APOCALYPSE

CLARISSA

Copyright © Karl Drinkwater 2021 (updated 2023)
Cover design by Karl Drinkwater. Interior illustrations by an AI.

Published by Organic Apocalypse
ISBN 978-1-911278-19-1 (E-book)
ISBN 978-1-911278-24-5 (Paperback)

Organic Apocalypse Copyright Manifesto

CLARISSA

BLACK AND CREAM

Blackness. It is not full black because some light shines through eyelids. They are thin skin, and light is so powerful it fights the dark and make swirls and whooshes of red-purple, which is just illuminated blood pumping. If you see the swoosh you must be alive.

I don't open my eyes.

The seat contains comfort-mould foam constructed of motile bubbles so tiny you could count them forever if you had super eyes, and still not get an accurate total. It wraps around me, all soft and warm.

I don't like it. I want my *old* chair, from my apartment with Opal. It was hard plasteen and did not mould and did not self-heat, and it wobbled because one leg was bent, making it three millimetres shorter than the others. I would swap this chair for that one in an instant. Less than an instant. Maybe three tenths of a second.

I feel the current seat beneath me and remember what it looks like, and in the blackness I *swap* it, and instead imagine I am sat on my old chair. And suddenly it *does* feel harder under my bum. I changed the world. I can do that, too. My big sister told me so.

I sit with my eyes closed in my hard chair and it's good. Though I can still hear *them*.

"I hate going under." Deep voice.

"Big man like you?" Woman's voice.

I won't open my eyes. There is nothing I want to see. Certainly not evil people in sharp-cut cream-coloured suits that almost match their skins. Anyway, in my head I can see more things than my eyes could ever show me.

I remember the layout around me, and picture it. Beyond the chair I sit on is a low table supporting three glasses, three drinks of different colours. Mine has one straw. The liquid is LemonFizz. It has no lemons in it and is not yellow. What it has is uncountable bubbles from carbonation. It is one of the basic elements of spicy taste alchemy. Fizzy is the spicy of air. Vinegar is the spicy of water. Chilli is the spicy of fire. Mint is the spicy of earth. Spicy taste alchemy. I made that up.

"Well, it's not fear, obviously ... I just don't like the lack of control in a full knockout. I'd rather have ten subcutaneous implants, without anaesthetic, than be put into a coma." Him.

"Don't have the procedure then." Her.

Beyond the drinks are the two people. Societal Services Agent Gloria Lefos (which she pronounces funny as "luhf-oh"), posh-voice-snatchy-arm-woman, age estimate: old, maybe twenty-nine. Also Societal Services Agent Aris Bradden, dark-hair-silly-muscle-man, age estimate: supermax old, maybe thirty-one.

"It took a long time to get into the top-tier credit category, I don't want to lose the privileges. And a free Monograd Dual-ventricle Cardiosystem Booster won't be a bad outcome."

"As long as you don't leave the service and have to return it."

I don't keep my eyes tight-squeezed shut because that is tiring. I just want the Agents to ignore me. They are horrible. They kidnapped me.

"Repo extraction's a myth." Corporate-lookalike-man Bradden.

"If you say so." Pale-skin-woman Lefos.

This atrium is a vast catering hall. Tables of different sizes everywhere, along with benches, staircases, curved seats, huge illuminated globes dangling from ceiling cables. Our table is one of the smaller, posher ones, where you have to go up steps to get to it, and you look down on everyone eating below.

I sit in whooshing darkness but there is lots of noise. The starship's lounge is huge, with people at every table, or stood in groups, or walking past us, all talking, all making a racket. There are announcements over the loudspeaker system, and the clinks of glasses, and footsteps, and the scraping of chairs, and a cough from a few metres away (a repeated cough, that person should cover their mouth). The sound echoes imply reverberation that matches the height of the ceiling which I calculated before I closed my eyes forever.

Some people serve and some are being served, food as well as drinks. One aroma might be pizza because there is a smell – sticky like cheese, hot like tomato, airy like dough – that brings new images to the darkness. Memories of lying on the floor with my sister and taking slices from the box, slices that are triangles but with one side convex-curved. That is a happy image and I can see it clearly, Opal smiling at me with strings of cheese stretched between her mouth and the pizza slice so that I laugh, because shapes can be twisted to new shapes which means the shapes don't follow rules. Or maybe they *do* but my sister is able to break the rules, which is also funny. We look alike but she is older, so that is what I will look like when I am four years older too, though she will have moved on by then. It is a race I cannot ever win, but because it is Opal and I love her I do not mind if she always comes first, and I just follow her. That smile of hers is better than the pizza. Move on, this hurts, internal belly twist like something torn from me, like a video of an operation which makes you scrunch your face up even though it isn't happening to you.

"I'll be glad when I can stop babysitting idiots and get back to my unit." Him.

"Shush." Her.

"The freak's asleep. The dose I gave her can cause secondary relapse. Still, civ-ships do have perks that mil-transports don't. We could go to the rec area next. There are aisles of gambling machines and a casino."

Other smells. There is a scent that might be something they wipe the tables with, a nose-stingy aroma of cleaner. And also the smell of people. It merges, and noses are not as accurate as eyes for distance and triangulation, but some people smell bad, and some smell clean. Grumpy-Agent-man has a smell of sweat but it is fresh, which is better than old sweat. The room is too warm for him. Many bodies in a room can affect the temperature. Pointy-nose-blonde-Agent Gloria Lefos has a different smell, it reminds me of acetone. I know the A-words well because when I last read through the Citizen Cyclopedia (the unlocked adult version, thanks to some cracking softs I found in Opal's data-store), I only got as far as acrylic acid, and recency is freshness. That is true whether you are considering memorised definitions, or old-people perspiration.

I prefer the first of those two things.

When these Evil Agents broke into our apartment with their security guard, a fight broke out. Opal told me to hide but I was too slow, and that is my fault. Opal did her best and hurt the armoured man with a heavy tool. She also el-bowed short-hair-white-skin-Agent-man in the face, making him bloody-nostril-black-eye-Agent-man, which I much prefer. Though he then became even-angrier-red-face-Agent-man, and he hurt Opal in return before they managed to cuff her wrists behind her back. Grabby-arm-Agent Gloria Lefos restrained me as I copied Opal's struggling and yelling (but not her bad words, because Opal always told me off if I copied those).

The point is, we fought, rather than surrendering with tears. Which is a funny reversal, in a way, because Opal had grabbed some CryBaby off the security guard's belt and sprayed it in his eyes, so that he ran to our bathroom to splash cold water on his face. The puffy red swollen eyes were an improvement. If his thin-skin eyelids would be closed for a day, so what? It's not so bad. I close mine all the time, I don't know what he was shouting about. He shouldn't have broken into our flat. He shouldn't have hurt my sister. They shouldn't have split us up.

Opal didn't want to be a soldier, but they said she has to be one. I don't want to go to Corporate Academy, but they said I have to. All because Mummy and Daddy are dead. Yet we were doing fine. Opal got me pizza and made noodles. I could play with RearroBlox as much as I wanted, as long as I did online school first. The high view of the other skytowers could be changed to anything I wanted when I closed my eyes.

We weren't harming anyone!

I did *try* to escape from the Evil Agents when we were boarding the ship, by *doing an Opal*. I kicked *him* in the shins and ran away, shouting that the Agents were evil kidnappers. I hoped one of the adults in the queue would help. But either they didn't believe me, or they didn't want to lose their place in the queue, because they all just watched with these big blank faces while he grabbed me (grown-ups have longer legs, that's not fair). I wriggled but *she* just held up ID and told everyone they were UFS agents, and he slapped some kind of sticky patch on my neck that knocked me out. By the time I woke up, dizzy with a dry mouth, we were already on the ship in our private suite. He was sat on a chair facing my bunk and she leaned against the wall with her arms folded. They both looked supermax serious.

"We're already in Nullspace," he'd said. "No getting off until the end. No escape. And so we have two choices. One: we can keep you in this room for the whole journey. That's no fun for anybody, because one of us has to stay here guarding you all the time. Cramped up with a smelly kid in this room is sure *not* my idea of fun."

"*I'm* not smelly. *You* are."

But he ignored what I said and carried on. "Or you can behave, and we can act like normal people, and smile, and explore the ship, and you don't try to run or scream or act like an animal. Deal?"

I didn't answer. Just copied the woman's posture, and folded my arms super-tight, to see how *he* liked it.

"I'll take silence as agreement. But just so you know, if you try *anything*, then it's straight back here. And, in case *that* sounds like fun ..." and here he held up a pouch, and it flipped open, revealing patches and liquid vials, "I'll use one of these on you and you'll be in a coma for the whole trip. I'm pretty good with sedatives, so it's unlikely to kill you, but ..." He shrugged.

And that's how I'm here as a hostage. The Agents wouldn't even tell me which of the ship's destinations is ours. I wish it was *them* who were dead instead of Mummy and Daddy.

And in this blackness that is really a whooshing swirl of blood and a universe where I can change things and create what I want, I cry out to Opal in my head. And I think I catch her calling back but it could be my tricky imagination, it sometimes makes me see things that Opal says aren't real, so who knows? Who knows? And it's faint, and far away, but if it *is* her then a line drawn between two points is the definition of a connection, so I feel calmer. I do not tense up my face in any way. I might look asleep on the outside, but I am *very* awake on the inside.

Oh yes.

My name is Clarissa. I am ten years old.

And they will all be sorry when my sister comes and rescues me.

SISTERS

ORANGE AND GREEN

Sound is sensation, tapping on a part of our ear which is so deep inside us you can't reach it even with a finger. So sound is really touch, just like some tastes have colour, and some smells have taste. A three-note chime bing-bongs through the air, louder than the voices and the clattering and the footsteps, and if grown-up announcements had a flavour it would be something like plastic.

"This is your captain, Andreas Kallaras," a deep voice announces, everywhere at once. "I hope you are having an exceptionally pleasant journey aboard the CC65 Solace. My crew are happy to assist with any requests. At hour twenty there's a maker's market and creative outlet performance in Concourse Four. If you wish to experience the singing, dancing, scaping and interactivities – or to take part yourself, if you possess an enactment skill – then I'm sure it will be an exciting diversion. With more than two thousand passengers, we have a lot of talent! The gambling zones are now available until we initiate synthetic nightphase. Also of note is that the transitional skywindows will open for an hour in the next few minutes, and – ah, excuse me, I'm needed on the bridge, but will continue this announcement later." Another triple bing, notes in reverse this time, and conversations start up again.

Operation-scaredy Agent-man Bradden prods me, and in surprise I accidentally open my eyes. It is headache bright, like a whole world of colours rushing into my head so fast it might just burst like the melon that time Opal triangulated microwaves as an experiment. Pieces of it dripped down the walls, supermax mess, and we laughed, but if Mummy and Daddy had been there we'd have been in trouble, and maybe that memory is sad after all.

"Had a good sulk?" he asks.

I don't answer him, or even *look* at him. He isn't worth it. I don't like looking at eyes anyway. Except for Opal's. I love looking at *her* eyes. But for now I squint at uncountable bubbles in LemonFizz, spicy of air. The drink was poured for me, even though I didn't ask for it. Why do grown-ups think kids like LemonFizz?

I *hate* LemonFizz.

Lemon is the stingy of acid. It makes faces scrunch up like tummy pain. That proves it is an evil ingredient. Even the fizz bubbles go up. They are trying to escape from the lemon.

"What about if we go to the skywindows, change of scene?" Agent Gloria Lefos asks me.

I do not look at her, either.

Her glass is empty. So is the man's.

"I think she's dumb." Him.

"She can talk." Her.

"All I've heard is animal screaming or petulant silence."

You can't hear silence. It is the absence of sound waves. He is the one who is dumb. I bet he never reads the Citizen Cyclopedia.

I don't stand up when they rise, so Agent Gloria takes my hand. Not tight enough to hurt, not like back at the apartment when she dragged me by the arm, but I won't be able to break free until she is distracted. *Then* I can run. *Then* I can hide. Lots of people to dodge around. I have a chance. I can't fight like Opal but I can be clever like she is. She would tell me to get away, and I failed last time, in our apartment, but I will succeed this time.

So I go with them. For now. I look down. My shoes rub. They are new, forced on me by the Agents. In the apartment me and Opal don't wear shoes, we have bare feet. Bare feet are grippy, tickly, not rubby. Shoes are foot prisons.

The floors are clean. Bots do it. Little ones that scoot about when there are not so many people, not so many feet, not so many shoes as I can see now. A bot would trip people up if it tried to clean at this minute. That would be hilarious. When grown-ups fall over it is funny. They look scared.

Clip clop go the shoes.

I fall over a lot when I play with Opal. It isn't scary. It makes me laugh. It makes Opal laugh. Sometimes falling over isn't the end of the game, it is just the start of another game, like the tickle game, which is a game that I hate and I love, like LemonFizz mixed with StrawberryFizz would be. If they made that thing. If you could buy it. LemberryFizz. StrawmonFizz. It would be a thing. People wouldn't know whether to scrunch up their faces or smile, and that would be a new thing too, a new face, a new expression, something closing in and expanding out at the same time. That is not stasis, it is something new, something that has no entry in the Citizen Cyclopedia yet.

Clip clop changes to thump thump on a carpeted area, then back to clip clop as we pass it.

When I grow up I plan to write new Citizen Cyclopedia entries. It will double in size. It will be called the Claripedia. It will be the best book in the world, available in all layers of connection, so if they choose "voice" it will be read out in Opal's voice, and if they choose "projection" it will be Opal's head and shoulders as well as voice, but under it all will be my words. I'll be rich, and I can buy a big apartment for me and Opal, and it will have power paid so Opal won't need to hack into the grids and risk electrocution, and no one will bother us ever. Certainly no Evil Grown-ups.

And we'll never wear shoes. Shoes are a grown-up idea. A posh pale-skin rich idea. A mean idea, designed to make blisters on kids' feet.

Clip clop.

I will write a new entry about shoes in the Claripedia. It will change people's minds. Shoes will stop being worn. They will be gathered up and sent to recyc, and made into toys.

We go up the escalator and I watch the grooves of the metal stairs connect and separate. I am pinned between the Evils. His shoes are black and shiny and show that he has big feet to match his muscles. Her shoes are black and shiny and she has smaller feet. His shoes have laces, hers do not. That is a strange thing. They are both Societal Services Agents, but maybe there are differences between them.

Classification systems require lists that summarise points of comparison. There are two types. Similarities, and differences. I like to categorise, because that is a required skill to write a Claripedia and be rich.

It is louder on this upper walkway which overlooks the concourse where we had drinks (or endured them and their bubbling lemon nastiness). All those voices, all those grown-ups being noisy, shouting, laughing – even though I bet they tell kids to be quiet! – it all echoes up here.

There is no escape on the left. Only a railing protecting you from a deadly fall, like when a sad jumper leaped from our skytower window because they had no money to buy food. You'd be splatted on the bot-polished floor down there, your head popped open like a microwaved melon.

On my right there are open alcoves for yet more social juice and alcohol bars, with their high stools and artificial plants. There are also shops. Not shops like me and Opal went to when we were hungry. These are tiny posh ones that sell useless stuff that costs more than it is worth. They are called boutiques. They sell clothes to people who already have clothes. They sell drinks like LemonFizz. They sell food. And shoes. And upgrades. And trinkets. And … toys.

That boutique has *toys*!

I don't care about most toys. The dolls and the guns and the interactive games and the puzzles and the models and the age-appropriate light shows. But that boutique has *RearroBlox*, the creative imaging toy.

I had a lot of them in our apartment, left behind with all our other stuff. Some were battered or chipped – the first ones

Mummy and Daddy bought me, before I learned to look after things better. A few had faded or damaged pix-displays. I looked at them closely and saw clusters of dead dots. But they all still worked. And the Blox let me talk to Freddie Bobo – just Bobo to his friends (me).

I stop walking.

I point at them, these things the Evil Agents had taken from me.

See them, I think; *see the RearroBlox.*

These are the new ones, that have better scenescapes and larger pictogram stores, and better algorithms for cross pollination, and smoother animation during the morph stage.

I wave my arm to indicate the display at the boutique's entrance. The whirling colours and pictures in their demo mode are much swirlier than thin-skin eyelid filters for concourse lighting.

"Why's she flapping her arm?" It is big-foot Agent Bradden who asks this in his deep voice. He speaks those words but he should really be saying, "I am sorry I took you away from your sister, it was a mistake, let me buy you all the RearroBlox to apologise, then I'll turn the passenger liner around and we'll take you back to Opal and make sad eyes because I know I was a Bad Man and am in trouble."

Instead, he shoves me. Just his hand, and maybe not seeming too hard for him, with his grown-up arms and muscles, but I don't expect it and nearly fall over. If Agent Gloria hadn't been holding my hand firmly I would have collapsed, and might have gotten my fingers trodden on by all the grown-ups pushing past, so that the squashed fingers would be sucked up by a cleaner bot when it next came along and I would look stupid with nothing sticking out of my palms.

"Hey!" says the woman. I thought she was shouting at me for pulling her, but she is not, she is shouting at the man because he pushed me. Big kids who push little kids are bullies, it's a definition, it's mine, and if I put a picture in the Claripedia for the bully entry it will be a picture of *him*.

I breathe fast and my chest goes deep up and down because this is one of the ways that I make the hurt go away, except it doesn't, not really, because it's still inside, but at least I don't let it get to my eyes, don't let him laugh at me for crying, so that he won't call me squirt. Because that's what bullies do, they call people names, too. It's not enough to just hurt your body.

And normally Opal would want to know why I breathe like this, and she would calm me down by hugging me and whispering nice stuff, her breath all tickly in my ear, and she might go and get revenge on the bullies; but she isn't here. She *should* be here.

We walk on, and I imagine shover-prodder Agent Bradden's head popping like a melon, because if that happens then I won't cry, no, I'll laugh, and laugh and laugh and laugh, because it will serve him right. I won't look at him. I won't let him see my eyes. They're *mine*. People can shove me but they can't look through my eyes and into my head.

If they tried to do that, they'd be oh so sorry.

Beyond the shops is an open area where the ship's exterior hull plating has slid back, so that the skywindows now show what is outside, rather than looking like pale-coloured wall when the panels are closed. We are on a tiled walkway suspended above the atrium, and to our right, past the safety railings, the skywindow is only ten metres away. This walkway is called a Vantage Point because the skywindow is so big that it drops out of sight below you and reaches up so high that it aches your neck to look at the top.

The walkway is packed with people staring through the clear plasteen at blackness: the word "transfixed" is the descriptor that I pick out from the word hoard.

"Just endless blankness," says Agent Gloria. "No stars. No obstacles. No friction."

"It's got no depth," says pusher-bully Agent Bradden. "Like a screen. There's no value or life in the black."

People nearby make similar comments.

They're all wrong. Grown-ups are often stupid. They don't ask questions like: if it's a screen, then what's it covering? They don't use their brains *or* their eyes properly.

I can see, though.

It's swirling, like the light through an eyelid. The same swoosh of near-matching colour. There is magenta in there, so dark it is *almost* black. There's a blue, the blue just before proper night, that deep blue that's clinging to the horizon in a lucky gap between skytowers. The colours ripple. Reminds me of fishies swimming, when we changed our apartment's Dornascreen to show aquarium scapes, before Opal changed it back to a display of a burning fireplace because it made us feel warmer. Fishies are many little bitty creatures, but some species are in groups that move and turn together, and then they become a single creature called a Shoal that reflects and shines as it turns around obstacles you can't even see, and makes decisions you can't understand.

There's definitely *something* out there.

Adults use their eyes all wrong. They think eyes are passive, like little lenses that just show one thing. But eyes are not passive. Adults just forget what they can do.

Sure, I can see what's there. But I can *change* it, too. If you hold up your hand with your fingers apart, you see five digits. If you look beyond your hand, they separate into ten blurs. You can then refocus, but only a little bit, and make some fingers overlap, and then you have a number that isn't five or ten, and some of the fingers look like solid brown, others like brown ghosts you can see through. It's the same as the trick you use to find the hidden images in a kid's Magic Focus book, where there are only squiggles and millions of coloured dots in layers, but if you concentrate you eventually find the right overlap of dots so some go solid, and instead of a mess of dots you see a shape floating in front of the screen, and if you're lucky it's a dolphin or a doggy; if you're unlucky it's a UFS logo or a gun.

I try it now, shifting focus amongst the vision-edge swirls, to make them overlap. But they dart about just when you think you have them. And then I notice the reflection of the Vantage Point in the skywindow, with all of us stood there, looking back at ourselves, from that world where things are the wrong way around but the shadows are perfect at copying us. And I see myself amongst them. I am easy to spot because the others nearly all have white faces, and mine is brown. In the reflection they resemble ghosts in a film, and I am the only one who looks real. It is the *other me*, ten metres outside the ship, stood in Nullspace, stillness amongst all the motion, intense and different. The reflection stares back from between bar-like safety railings, and she is as much a prisoner as I am.

Her lips move. She tries to tell me something. I wonder if that means my own lips are moving, but I don't think they are. I can't hear what she says, because the skywindow is in the way. And anyway, out there is vacuum, and sound can't travel in vacuum. So I hold up a hand and wave, and she waves back. I point at my ear and shake my head, and she does the same. She understands.

We can use Longping Code to communicate. If you don't have a beeper or a flasher you can hold up your open palm. A rotation of the wrist is short ping. A fist is long ping. Separate the fingers for the end of the word. That is the simple form.

I am gesturing "Hello" when Nosy Agent Bradden asks what I'm doing. I ignore him and keep signing but he grips my arm and lowers it. I try to resist but his evil makes him strong. I begin to use my other hand but he twists me away from the skywindow, to face him. I look down so he can't see into my eyes.

"She was signalling someone," he says, not to me. "Scan the area." But then I know he is talking to me when he leans in and speaks in a low voice that is nasty, like a troll. "Do you know why they open the windows a few times a day?"

I ignore him. His big white hand hurts my wrist.

"It's because of a special illness people have. A kind of space claustrophobia on long journeys through Nullspace, where they feel trapped. It's also why some walkways have screens showing fake views as if we're flying through clouds, or in a ground vehicle with the land rushing by. Nutjobs can go there to calm down. So why not just leave the skywindows open all the time, I hear you say – or I would, if you weren't so dumb you can't talk. Well, that's because of the *opposite* illness, another thing that affects us, and even some animals. Staring at the blackness of Nullspace can drive weak people mad. And no one even knows why. They stare. And stare. And stare. Kind of intense, like you. And then they flip, and hack other people apart with an axe, or they poison them, or they rip out their own eyes. Sound familiar? That's why I'm going to keep a close eye on you, and you're not to try anything like signing for help. Right?" He shakes my arm when I don't reply. "Say something, you frizzy freak. I'm talking to you!"

Now he really hurts me, even though I can avoid showing it.

So I look at him. Right in his Evil Agent little blue eyes. With satisfaction I note the pink bulge on his nose where hardened nano-skin is still slowly repairing the broken bone underneath: the fracture a well-earned present to him from my sister.

"Anaesthetic is a lie," I tell him. "It is supposed to have two effects. *Unconsciousness*, and *paralysis*. That enables surgeon-bots to cut us open and change parts or slice out bad stuff and stitch us up again. But it does not do *those* two things. Instead it causes *paralysis* and *memory loss*. That is why some doctors claim we don't really understand how it works. It is a grand lie they have to uphold, because if they didn't then people would never have operations, and more people would die. So they agree to hide the truth in order to save lives. Because saving lives is a medical priority two levels above preventing suffering. But the truth is that anaesthetic paralyses the body so an operation can take place, but the patient is fully conscious. They feel everything. Then the memory fades as paralysis wears off, and life carries on. But the psychology part of the Citizen Cyclopedia says that

we have portions of the brain which are subconscious and remember things, and try to warn us. And people who've had an
operation before are uneasy about having another because *their
subconscious knows*. It *remembers*. It screams at them not to do
it. But grown-ups don't listen to the screaming, because then
other grown-ups might call them nutjobs and freaks. So they go
through the torture again, and feel every slice, every scrape, every
gash."

It is strange. His skin is normally kind of pinky-yellowy, like
people who have lots of money and big castles to live in and
maybe eat cake for every meal. And yet, it whitens while I talk
to him. I changed his skin colour just by making sounds that
go in his ears. And he can't take his eyes off me, which maybe
means I've hypnotised him, which would be a cool thing because
I always wanted to hypnotise people ever since I read about it,
but whenever I tried it on Opal to get her to let me stay up late,
it never worked.

"I'm not dumb," I finish, snatching my arm back: his hand is
so floppy it's like his big muscles have gone to sleep.

His mouth is a bit open and floppy too, which is not nice,
because he ate some food earlier and a green bit is stuck between
his teeth. And his staring eyes seem bigger, too. I'm not sure why.
I need to go back to the Cyclopedia's biology sections. I don't
like those wide eyes, so point at his palm, because I know he has
an imager implanted under the skin there.

"Why don't you scan my contours?" I ask him. "It would last
longer." That's something Opal says when mean men stare at
her, but it sounds cooler when she does it.

And I kind of regret it when he slaps my face, snapping my head to the side and knocking my gaze from him.

Agent Gloria steps between us, one hand on my shoulder to keep me behind her, as if she's become my shield.

"What's the matter with you, Bradden?" she snaps at him. "You're acting like an amateur!"

He stands up, and because he's taller, he looks down on both of us. "And I've no idea why you're taking an interest for once," he answers with a kind of doggy snarl. "That's not like *you*, Lefos."

The people around us back away from the confrontation. Maybe they noticed the same thing I did: he is clenching his fists. But he doesn't use them. Instead, they relax, and the anger fades so that he looks pale again, somehow smaller. "I hear they've got cumd— ... erm ... SynthMate boudoirs on this damned ship. Might as well enjoy the privileges, while you play mother witch."

The nearest people make way for him as he strides off.

Gloria-possible-witch-woman says, "Disgusting," under her breath.

I'm only ten but my cracked Cyclopedia, which includes content normally blocked from kids, has an entry on SynthMates. I've read it. And I agree with Gloria.

Agent Gloria squats in front of me and tries to look into my eyes but I won't let her, not now. I stare down at her smaller black shiny shoes where the hem of her cream-coloured trouser suit brushes them.

"Are you okay?" she asks.

I wonder if her feet are the same colour as her hands. My feet have two different shades, top and bottom, but I'm not sure about hers.

"He was wrong to hit you."

The ship lights flicker. It's so subtle I don't think anyone else notices. Again, grown-ups are rubbish at using their eyes. It's a wonder they can do anything without tripping over their useless shoes.

"You're not a freak," she says.

I don't care. Not that she speaks posher than me and Opal and the people in our skytower. Nor that the ship is full of people like her. I *know* I'm different from all of them. I have eyes that I actually *use*.

"Let's go back over here," she says, "see if there's anything that will cheer you up."

And there's no point her pretending to be nice, that's just what grown-ups do, pretend: important people on the news saying they care about something when none of it's true, none of it touches their eyes. She can buy me all the OrangeFizz on the ship and I *still* won't be her friend.

She takes my hand and leads me anyway. Everyone else is back to normal, staring out of the skywindows at their reflection selves. I wonder how many of them wink back, and wave, and try to tell their doubles the secrets?

I like secrets.

I like knowing other people's.

But, even more than that, I like having my *own*.

And I expect Agent Gloria to offer me a drink, or even noodles, but instead she stops at the only good boutique, so maybe she does sometimes use her eyes and connect what she sees with her brain after all.

There are boxes and shiny vehicles and moving things and screens and animations, but it's the display pile I look at, the swooshing pictograms that merge and spread between cubes, dumb random because it's demo mode but hinting at the possibilities of what you can do if you've focussed on them for most of your life.

She must notice what I'm gazing at.

"RearroBlox?" she asks. "Aren't you a bit old for them?"

I put my free hand on the glass of the display case.

"Okay. RearroBlox it is."

She leads me to the counter. My palm left a sticky handprint on the glass, like a reflection, aligned so that I see through it to the twenty-six demo Blox. It's as if they are already mine, marked by my fading trace, guaranteeing that the world will map to my intentions.

Then again, even if I imagine something clearly, my hands can't always shape it properly in putty. It is frustrating when the proud lion of my mind looks like collapsed sausage noodles in my hand.

A minimal set of RearroBlox is four. Common is nine. Sixteen if you are lucky. I used to have nineteen, because Mummy and Daddy got me extra ones from Father Festivalue.

Gloria buys a set of nine. That is still good, especially as they're the newer ones. I haven't ever tried this iteration. I wish I could combine them with the ones left in my apartment – new Blox are always compatible with old.

The Blox are placed in a carry bag with pellets of Squish Biofoam to keep them from banging together. I want to get them out now, put them on the floor and sit with them, but maybe-not-so-bad Gloria leads me outside, and I am glad just to hold the bag tight against me with my other arm. I won't let anyone leave *these* behind.

"Let's go and sit down," she says. "But there's a condition. You'll need to talk to me, tell me about yourself. Deal?"

I nod. With grown-ups, you have to nod. If you won't deal, then they take things away from you.

We sit at a table nearby. It's on a raised platform and has a good view of the skywindows, and the slick black thing we're sliding along in Nullspace, with all the textures behind it that the grown-ups say they can't see.

"You can try them out here," Gloria says, "but you need to stick to our agreement."

I don't like to talk much. But Opal taught me lots of things. One of them is to adapt to a situation. *Quickly*. Opal doesn't force me to talk, because she loves me, and wants me to be happy: but I can talk if I have to. I can let one part of my brain do that. It pretends to be me pretty well. It's not the part where I live, though. When I do this, grown-ups think they are talking to me, when really they are talking to a drawing book, not the me that is *doing* the drawings.

"Tell me things about your life with your sister," she suggests.

"I can think of four," my autoresponder says. "They are not all good, but most."

I take each block from the bag and lay it on the table, careful to peel off any squishers that have stuck to them, like bubbly slugs, and drop those back into the bag. RearroBlox are cubes where each face is a screen that can display moving images. The images are altered by the other images on the cubes *around* them, and the way they are all positioned. If you have a cube displaying a yellow circle, another with a green square, a third with a tree, and one with a sort of grassy texture, then put them together, they might merge so that all become wooded hillsides with sun shining down. You can separate images again in the same way.

Each of these new Blox is in standby, showing the swirl pattern. I pick up a cube, shake it, and look at the six sides: abstract, tree, a word, a rotating star, part of a face, bubbles. Then repeat, and repeat again, noting which of the images are new ones, until I find the seed I want. It's a green hill. I centre it and let go, so that the cube's other five sides switch off, then pick up another cube and shake it to give six different options, looking for the correct predominant colours or textures. Lines like hairs, blue of a sapphire that spins, and so on. I put them in the right places, occasionally tapping one on another to merge content to the correct amount based on proximity. If you keep your hands on them you can keep altering the distance before finalising a creative mix on the upper faces, and then the pink and white colours slide over them to finalise the current top pattern and turn off the other sides.

"Go on, then," she says.

"A slopy set of walkways circled our skytower. I used to go up and down them on a wheelboard. That was brilliant. There were pink and white paving panels, and moss on the wall. Opal watched me in case I fell off, or big kids came along."

Maybe the finalisation colours don't slide so much as *wash* over the panels, like water?

"Another thing I remember was that my bed was wet when it rained sometimes, because the window above it wouldn't shut properly."

Blox finalise the top image (and turn off the other panels) when you let go, but as long as you keep hold of them they display all six sides. There is a legend that any side you can't see will actually display a demon's face if it is after midnight: and if you look at it, you die. It's not true. I tried it one night with a mirror and it wasn't a demon's face, it was just a continuation of the image. Some people are such liars.

"That sounds bad."

"Yes, I didn't like the wet. But I wouldn't let Opal move my bed because I liked to look at the moons when I was in bed at night, reflecting in my mirror. If it got too wet then Opal let me sleep in her bed, with her, in the room next door. That was good, too. If I had a real doggy I wouldn't have minded a wet bed, but I never had one so Opal was next best."

I keep rearranging content that expands from the options in my seed image, and soon it might look like a mess to others, but *I can see it*. In the dots, there is green, a small shape in the background, it is fur. It is Bobo. My doggy. He is three centimetres tall, and has orange eyes and green fur. After Opal, he's my best friend. He has always been in the Blox, and when I'm tired and stare at them for a long time, he gets clearer, and changes among the pictures, breaking up and reforming with the transformations, but always in there somewhere, even when he is sometimes spread across Blox in bitty parts and swirls. It doesn't hurt him to get split and recombined, he told me. After Mummy and Daddy died he could talk louder.

Opal can't see him. She is too grown-up.

"A third thing," says Gloria.

I glance at her and notice her eyes are brown, like Opal's, even though Gloria has blonde hair. "Okay," I reply, pretending to think for a moment, as if I'm really paying attention. "You know that chocolate spread that's got white and brown bits in? I had that every day for months."

These Blox are higher-res, and Bobo winks at me, his orange eye hidden as a fruit on a green tree, and his fur expands as a landscape on the nearby Blox, sticking up like sharp claws.

"Hello, Clarissa," he says.

"Hello, Bobo." I reply in my head, as Bobo always insists, so no one else can hear us.

"I thought you were avoiding me."

"No. They made me leave you behind."

"That isn't healthy." Gloria crosses her legs. Kids never sit like that. But her legs *are* long.

"Opal let me. Well, mostly. Sometimes I snuck into the kitchenette at night and scooped some with my finger. And Opal only let me have it if I ate all my dinner. That meant anything flavoured like fruit or veggies, too. But I definitely had it more than when Mummy and Daddy were alive. Opal was even nicer to me after that."

"It would be bad to leave me. I'd be very, very upset." Bobo was hiding in a bush image and speaking from there.

"Your voice is different. Less friendly. More scratchy."

"It's an echo chamber out here. Nullspace does that. Woof."

"And your eyes aren't just orange any more, they keep changing colour."

"Don't worry, I'm just testing out the latest gen of Blox. New anim effects!"

"Is that four things?" asks Gloria.

"No. It was three." I don't like Bobo's new voice, it resembles insect legs rattling in a tube. "The other thing was in second summer. There were always these big crawlies, Mossareid Decapedes, they did a migration. Most of them wouldn't bite, but some of the biters looked similar to the non-biters, making it hard to tell them apart. Sometimes the crawl swarm would pass through skytower residence zones. They got sprayed dead in posh low-rise areas, but not in ours. So you'd look out your window and see all this black on another skytower, but it wasn't shadow, and it wasn't mouldy, and it wasn't black paint: it was the migrating Decapedes. And I worried they were on *our* skytower, too. The Decapedes were long-legged ones, the worst ones. At those times, when it was super hot and your hands and feet got sweaty because the environmental controls were busted again, I wouldn't go into my room where the window was broken unless Opal went first and checked *everything*, even under the bed. That's horrible, isn't it?"

"They took Opal away, Bobo."

"I know. We need to call her."

"Can we do that?"

"Sort of. I have some friends that can. Sandmen. They aren't scary."

"Yes, enough to give you nightmares," says Gloria.

"Oh, I never get *those*. Well, hardly ever. Can I take off these shoes? They're really rubbing me sore."

"To call Opal you need to follow my lead. The patterns I'll take you through. The key thing is the shapes, much more than the colours. Or rather, the relationship BETWEEN the shapes. Nine Blox is a small grid, so the overall complex patterns you need to learn are heavily abstracted. So we subdivide them by careful manipulation of interior content. A triangle gives us three extra node points. A multi-faceted shape gives many more. The alignments, movements, and timings need to be right, but even when they're wrong they can have some effect."

I follow his suggestions whilst also talking to Gloria, and switch, switch, merge. I'm used to this. We have many configurations, some of them we named, like the Cross-hill Patch, or the Deep-fall Speckle, and over time we find new ways to get into that configuration. Some of them are ones we found by accident, some are ones Bobo has led me to when he points with his waggy tail or panty tongue. We go on adventures, making up stories for the images as we travel away from Realspace for hours at a time until it's confusing when it ends and I remember that it wasn't real.

Right now we've entered one of the geometric branches so it is much easier to get shapes, and I still see Bobo amongst them in the green glint, or the base of a prism that becomes his new swirling-coloured eye, or the texture of the polyhedron orbital which looks like burnished steel at one angle, and green fur at another.

The shapes interlock between the Blox, and glow, and I am surprised at some of the possibilities which we're creating, they are much more advanced and directable than usual.

"It's like a cheat code, unintentional exploits we can use by getting the timing, proximity and combination JUST RIGHT."

"Okay," says Gloria. "Since we're sitting."

I pause shuffling the Blox, undo the catches, and use my toes to push off each heel and let the shoes drop.

"There's a water channel near our skytower. We went there when it was hot. We used to paddle in the water and call it a stream. Someone threw an apple in and their doggy went in after it! The dog was diving and getting anything they threw in, at the deeper parts."

I snatch off the socks.

"Mmm, smell these, lovely. If you get up early in the morning, and want to wake someone like a big sister, then if you put a dirty sock on their face they'll get up. You could try it with that horrible man you work with. But look at my foot."

I lift my leg so she can see the bottom of it. She holds my ankle and peers closely, but it is not a tight grip now, not like when she grabs my arms sometimes. This is more like holding an insect to look at it before you let it fly away again.

"When I was paddling one time my foot got sliced bad on some broken glass that I hadn't seen under the water."

"Ouch. I can see the scar."

"Opal stitched it up, and she made it not hurt much at all."

I get my leg back. Bobo is making me rotate some Blox to specific angles, an interface option I don't normally use.

"See, this is a communication key that my friends can boost."

When he smiles now, within a cube, it looks like he has more teeth than usual.

"What we're doing now is repeating but speeding up."

And it is true, that my fingers go faster. I do not need to think so much when Bobo helps me. I allow him to use my hands. I am in control, though. I can stop him if I want. At least, he has always told me that.

"Ideally you need to get this cycle blocked in, then attach the Blox to a charging point. Data and electric networks are separate but they overlap in the control synapses, otherwise there'd be no shut off or redirection systems. I can call through those to other parts of the ship."

"What will that do?"

"It just means we can reach the communications arrays and send a message. Woof. A lovely message, because it will tell Opal where we are, like leaving a light on at night, and even though we are in Nullspace she will hear it, she will come for you."

"Can she get here, though?"

"Let Bobo worry about that. You charge me up, you memorise these patterns so you can make the picture shapes in your head. That's how we help Opal. That's how you escape. Woof."

"I don't know, Bobo. You're behaving funny."

"I told you, just Null effects, you are – woof! Woof! Waggy tail! Sad eyes?"

Tables all have standard charging points. I slide one of the Blox above the transference plate, which will automatically begin the recharge process on anything with a compatible interface that's placed there.

"You are so fast at those," says Gloria. "I've never seen anything quite like it. I can't even tell what those images are meant to be."

"It's a pointillising effect, one of the abstraction systems. The selection has created a delay with ghosting, often used for firework animations but teased out from the source. I touch the pattern, and the pattern touches me. It's tricksy, and I couldn't do it without Bobo."

"Bobo?"

"No, don't tell her about me. You know what grown-ups are like! She would think you are lying, and punish you by taking the Blox away."

He's right.

"Bobo is just the name for the combo I use to get into geometric branches from the landscape seed. I learnt it when I was little, and it helped me remember the sequence of back, onwards, back, onwards."

Bobo laughs. "Humans are so gullible," he says. It sounds like a nasty laugh to me, and Bobo is normally nice.

"Don't be mean," I say.

"Oopsie, sorry." He sounds more goofy now, but the scratchy voice will take time to get used to.

"Still, I'm impressed," Gloria tells me. "And sometimes, talking to you, it reminds me of a phrase my mother used."

"What?"

"'An old head on a young body'. Like what you said to Bradden about anaesthesia."

I don't move the Blox any more. Bobo is finished.

"Have you spoken to Opal, Bobo?"

But he doesn't respond. The Blox just have the glowing shapes, the dots rotating like locks. His new hi-res swirly colour eyes don't wink at me any more. His Null-echoing scratchy voice has stopped, too. He's gone. *Somewhere else.*

He does that sometimes.

I think he gets bored with me.

I tap each block two times, and they reset to default readiness patterns. I can't wait until Opal gets my messages and comes for me.

"I'm a bit hungry," I say, adapting to my new way of acting, of pretending to be a different Clarissa.

"Shall we go and get some food?"

"Yes. Noodles."

Noodles is a funny word. One of those that looks funny when you write it, curly like the food, but also *sounds* funny. If I had a doggy, a real dog, I might call it Noodles. It wouldn't have a scratchy voice like the new Bobo, it would have a huffy voice that is all waggy and panty. Instead of a winking and swirling eye it would have a wet nose, and the new dog would be a big one, up to my waist, not only finger-sized like Bobo.

Noodles *is* a funny word. But I stop thinking that when my Blox wobble on the table. People nearby grab railings on the walkway as the ship kind of lurches to the side. Nullspace is meant to be super smooth.

Then the lights flicker. Not just the ones near us, but every light across the concourse, even the hidden ones that shine up or down walls. One or two stifled shrieks break out before the lights come back to full strength.

Bing bing bong. An announcement. "This is the Chief Mate speaking. The captain is busy but asked me to reassure you all. We are having some engineering issues, all minor, so don't worry. This class of ship has numerous failsafes for every system. There's nothing dangerous about the slight shifts of gravity, it's tied to energy pulses as cells release excess charge."

Even as he speaks, the ship vibrates. Drinks on nearby tables wobble across the surfaces, towards the edge where they'll spill and fall.

"Again, please don't worry. I have to go, there will be an update soon."

He says the last bits very quickly. They do not sound calm.

And as I look beyond the people at the skywindow, I notice that the view has changed.

"Can you see that?" I ask, pointing.

"What? Nullspace?"

"Not just that. The swirling out there is faster than before, seems angry. There are pulses and holes in the deeper bits, can't see them properly, kind of blocked by cloud."

She stares at the areas I point to, but shakes her head. "It's all blank to me."

"I'm telling the truth," I say.

She looks down at me, and I don't look away this time.

"I believe you," she replies.

There's another vibration, and then the lights go out completely.

REARROBLOX ARE NOT TOYS

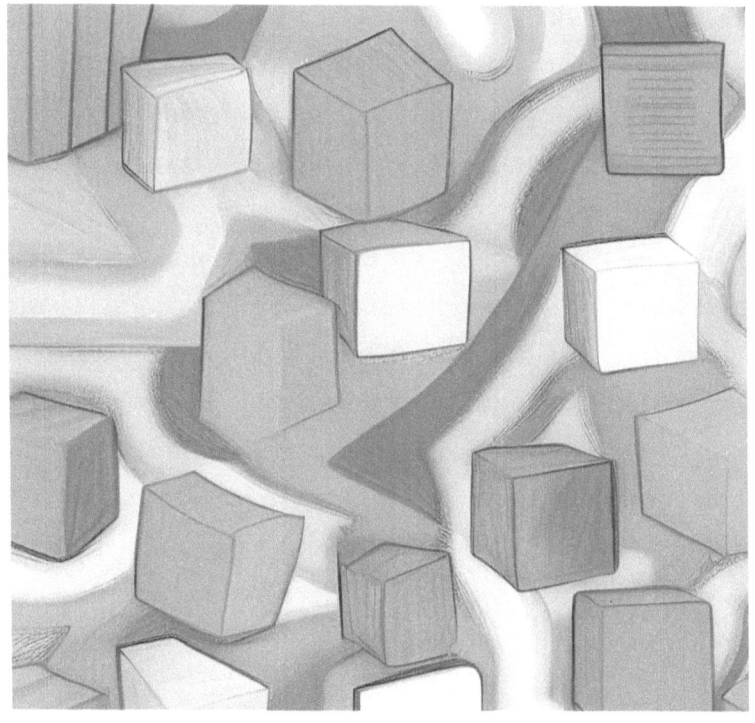

BLUE AND WHITE

Darkness isn't so bad to me, I've never been scared of it. Which is funny, because grown-ups always think kids *are* scared of it, and the adults act all brave ... but it's the grown-ups who make the scared noises right now.

Lighting comes back but it is faint emergency lights. Blue arrows on the floors point towards gathering points, and exits are illuminated in glowing red rectangles.

Bing bing bong. "This is the Chief Mate again, we're still experiencing issues, but will soon have it under control. In the meantime, if you have a cabin, please return to it immediately. If not, then head for the nearest LAS bank, and strap yourself into the Launch And Sleep seats. Please stay calm and act in an orderly manner. All crew are to close recreational facilities and assist passengers. This is *not* an emergency, just a ... precaution. Thank you for your cooperation." *Bong bing bing.*

Gloria activates some gadget implanted under the skin of her wrist and speaks into it.

"Bradden, same where you are? Yes. Get back up here. No, meet at our suite. Check."

While she's talking I put the RearroBlox in my bag, not forgetting the one from the transference plate interface. I also drop my shoes and socks in there before she makes me put them back on.

If she notices, she doesn't say anything.

We hold hands and follow the walkway towards the nearest group of elevators. Most people are not being calm like the Chief said. They jostle and push around us, trying to reach the exits first. Gloria keeps me nearby, using her free arm to shove anyone who gets too close. She seems strong, and I squeeze her hand tighter so I'm strong too. Still, it looks like it will be some time before we get to the front of the crowd.

"We'll use the staff elevators," she says, changing direction towards one of the boutiques just as the shutters at the front start to lower. We duck under them as they rattle down. This is one of the clothes shops, with mannequins wearing billowy dresses and flouncy tops. I like my clothes tight, same as Opal. Then they don't get caught on handles and railings, or trip you up if you're running.

"Won't we get in trouble, coming in here?"

"No. Special privileges of my job," she says with a wink, leaning over the shop counter and holding her palm against a scanner to cancel the automated trespass warnings that had begun when the boutique's AI detected us.

Earlier, the harsh shop lights burned everywhere, making colours brighter, shining through material to turn walls into rainbows. Now it is shadows, with only enough light to make out the dark shapes of obstacles, and where your feet go on the floor. Before, the blank-faced dummies stretched arms out in silly poses, like fashionistas. Now, they look like they're reaching out to grab us.

At the back of the shop is a staff door. It was almost invisible earlier, looking the same as the wall panels, but now it's outlined in red light. It slides up when Gloria touches the recessed controls, revealing a narrow corridor. I expected more people to be rushing around, but it's dead quiet. And even darker than the shop. There's only a single light every few metres. It's blue, and makes the passage seem cold, like a bottom-lit swimming pool.

Gloria checks something on her wrist and leads us to the right.

"Is that a Comm-Bond?" I ask.

"Yes. In my job we have them implanted under the skin, along with the connected palm scanners."

"I read that they have filament wires that run alongside the bones to connect to your nervous system."

"That's true."

"It's a bit gross." I walk closer to her every time we pass through the dark patches between blue lights. If anything stood there, we wouldn't know until we bumped into it.

"It's not the worst procedure. I've had more painful modifications. Never mind that, though. The important thing is that we're away from the crowds, and you're not going to get your little toes trodden on."

"Oh, you noticed."

"Sure I did, you barefoot bandit. But we were in a hurry so that was quick thinking on your part. Well done."

I smile up at her. She is looking ahead, watching the shadows as carefully as I was a moment ago. Maybe I could be an Agent. Not some horrible one that kidnaps kids, but maybe a secret one, or a rebel one.

"I can grip better with my toes."

"Isn't the floor cold?"

"No, it's quite hot."

She kneels and puts a hand there, then looks at something on her wrist display. It's invisible when the screen is inactive, so she just has normal-looking skin; then when it lights up the skin goes transparent, as if there's no covering at all.

"You're right," she says, as we move on. "Underfloor heating panels? Anyway, the map says there's not far to go. The maintenance corridor should have a staff elevator soon, and we can go straight to our deck."

"Did you hear that?" I ask, stopping, so that Gloria stops too. She listens.

"No, what?"

"Swishing noises. Behind us. When we walked."

"I don't hear anything."

"It was like rustly clothes. Or when the breeze blows rubbish along the pavement." And I picture one of the shop dummies following us, walking when we walk, stopping when we stop, just out of range of the blue light ... and I really wish I hadn't thought of that.

She grabs my hand and we continue, but backwards this time. Nothing jerks into the blue lights. Nothing visible pursues us. Then we turn and walk more quickly towards the elevator.

"Maybe you imagined it?" she suggests. Though I notice she speaks more quietly than before.

So do I. "Maybe. I do have a good imagination. Opal said so."

Except, sometimes, I don't think it is my imagination. Just because other people don't see what I see, doesn't mean it's not there. My eyes are better than theirs.

And my ears, too. Because I'm sure there's a clacking noise again. In the blackness behind us.

It could be the pipes. Or a cleaning bot somewhere.

It could be.

There's a red glow ahead. To the left side of the passage. We are almost running now. That's scary, because it makes it hard to hear anything behind, but there's also a good part to it. It means Gloria believes me.

Gloria slaps the call button, and the doors slide open immediately. Inside the capsule it is dimly lit, emergency lighting there too, but it's brighter than the corridor and I'm grateful to step inside with Gloria. We face the door, and the darkness beyond, and it seems all too long before it hisses shut, an angry hiss, and I keep expecting a stiff arm to jab out of the shadows and stop the door from closing.

When that doesn't happen I breathe normally again. The door is closed, the display beeping its way through deck numbers. And although another tremor vibrates the ship, so that it tingles in my feet, I am glad to be out of that service area corridor.

Maybe I should be scared of the dark after all.

We step out of the capsule, onto our deck. As with the other floor, it is only lit by emergency lights, just enough to direct you without distractions, and prevent you from bumping into anything. When all you can see is arrows and a route, people don't waste time looking at fake plants and pictures and boutiques and fizz dispensers.

This corridor has small windows to the outside. But, instead of blackness, there's turquoise light coming in, and I'm not the only one who can see it this time. It washes over the walls opposite the viewports, and the faces of the people crowding to look out. At least this corridor is not as crammed as the big skywindow concourse was. Or maybe the darkness just makes it seem like people have thinned out, because you can't see so far ahead.

"We must have dropped back into Realspace," someone says.

Gloria whispers, "That's not Realspace."

Beyond the five centimetre-thick transparent plasteen is an endless fog of luminous greenish blue clouds, all swirling together like a photo of a nebula where you've messed with the gain and vibrancy until it becomes unreal (but makes a fun background for the Dornascreen in my apartment).

Partly hidden in that churning mass are translucent clusters. I can't tell if they are ball-sized and in the nearby aqua mist, or if they are far away and as big as a planet. They are lumpy, irregular, like a tumour (tumours need to be identified early on and reported to a doctor). Some of them have bits peeling away, like strands or skin tears, and these reach towards other blobs, connecting them like tiny filaments.

It's beautiful.

I look up at Gloria but she is frowning, as if it isn't a good thing. Her face is all bluish green too, reflecting the cloudsky outside. Because her skin is nearly white she reflects the colour properly. I hold up my arm but it doesn't look the same on my skin, it just becomes a darker teal, none of the shades she shows. If you put us together, maybe you would get the widest range of turquoise, and it could be a good piece of teamwork, rather than each of us only being a partial reflection of that wonder outside.

But we leave it. Gloria pulls me. Not hard, but I have to go with her.

The floor here has a kind of carpet in the centre of the hall, soft on my toes. It is bouncy and would be fun to skip on if we weren't moving so quickly, heading for the next set of blue arrows. They are on the upper surface in this section, instead of embedded in the floor. It feels like we're running on the ceiling. You can do that with artificial gravity, I think. I've always wanted to try it.

The next junction takes us to an open area, an LAS bank of Launch And Sleep seats. It's where poorer people without private rooms can strap into comfy chairs during acceleration and deceleration. Controls let them face different angles and slope backwards so the seats can become beds, too. The heated seat foam makes them cosy, and a hood extends over your head so it's dark inside for sleeping. I'd have enjoyed them, but we do have our own rooms, because Gloria and Nasty Agent Bradden must be a kind of royalty. They got treated differently from other people at the boarding station. They skipped queues and didn't have to go through body scanners. They were even assigned a UFS status suite.

Our suite has two sets of bunk beds. I have one to myself, on the opposite side of the room to them. I picked the bottom one, because it has a curtain I can close so that I'll pretend I am not kidnapped, but am at home with Opal, and I am just hiding under our table and Opal has let me dangle a sheet over it that reaches down to the ground. I like to play with my RearroBlox under the table tent at home, and because it's darker, the colours on the Blox seem brighter. That's when I first met Bobo. He is shy, so usually only appears when there is no one else around. He was definitely acting funny earlier.

Lots of people are strapping into the seats, each one illuminated from below by pale white emergency lighting. The ship rumbles again, which encourages everyone to clip in faster, while me and Gloria rush through the area, heading for the blue-lit shadows on the other side.

There are no windows in this concourse. And yet, there *is* blue-green light here. Others notice it at the same time as me, and the sight affects everyone differently, because some people moan, and some sigh, and some whimper.

It's one of the lumpy clusters I'd seen in the outside clouds. Its size is clear now, as it floats higher up in this reclining chamber, strands reaching off through walls and ceilings, like stretched cables. I wonder if they reach towards other clusters of lumps. The mass is about three metres in diameter at the widest point, though the lumpiness gives it an irregular shape. The nodules are textured, making it look old. And as it drifts in front of emergency lights I can see the lights *through* it, like the cluster is not really fully here. Or maybe it isn't moving at all, we are, and the Solace is somehow passing through one of these lumps. Yes, it could be us that are the ghosts here.

It isn't moving fast, but it is steady, and is halfway down towards one area of reclining seats when people spot the slanted trajectory and panic and unclip themselves to get out of the way. Everyone's now lit up in peaceful aquamarines. If I can have a new top and shorts to replace the ones I'm wearing, I'd like them that colour, maybe self-illuminated fabrics with animation. Then I could be like a walking cluster, and go through walls, and get back to Opal a lot easier. Or at least hide from Agents whenever I want.

"This makes no sense," says Gloria, who has stopped, because our route coincided with the knotty mass.

"It's pretty, though. It might be someone's home. Or a nest," I tell her.

For some reason, that makes her look even more worried.

Bing bing bong. "... calm, this is outside our ... mustn't ... trying to ..." and the fractured voice just stops, without even the *bong bing bing* of goodbye. Instead, a huge groan echoes throughout the ship, and I wonder if it is the teal strand-connected cluster that's come out of the clouds, or if it is some huge monster shouting and angry somewhere on another deck. It could even be hull stresses – I know about vehicle construction, it was one of my favourite topics a few months ago.

The cluster is closer to the seats now. It will pass them and disappear through the floor, to the deck below. One person is having trouble with his belt, still in the chair, and no one goes to help him, they are all backing away – or running away – from the greenish blue mass, even if it is only made of light that looks like glass. The lines that come out from it ripple, so maybe they aren't rigid, and as other lumps – on other decks, I guess – move, they stretch or shorten. I wonder if lumps in other places are bigger, and this is a baby one? Babies *do* scream.

Except it isn't the pod-thing that's screaming, it's the person who's still strapped into the chair, and even when the cobalt blue lump passes through the floor and out of sight, leaving just glowing filaments behind, which hardly give out any aqua light, the man is still screaming, and I wonder if the cluster reached out and touched him in some way. He thrashes in the seat. Gloria tries to pull me away.

"We should help him," I say, resisting. "Opal said to treat people how *you* want to be treated." Gloria ignores me, and is powerful enough to drag me a few steps. "Plus, we need to know what's going on," I add. She pauses. I finish with, "It might help us," and it's enough persuasion.

She changes direction and we join the few other people who gather around the man, though no one wants to go too close to him. He's stopped screaming now, which is good, because it was scary, but he jerks within the straps like he's being electrocuted in a cartoon. The way the white emergency lights below the seat shine upwards makes people's faces look scary, with shadows in the wrong places, eyes black holes.

"Any of you medics?" asks Gloria.

The monsters shake their heads.

"Great. I'm the most qualified."

She doesn't really mean it is great. It's called irony.

Gloria kneels down to my level. "I'll see what I can do, as long as you stay back and promise not to run. Deal?"

I nod.

Gloria squats by the man.

A nod isn't the same as a promise. We didn't spit in our palms and shake on it, or circle our hearts.

She puts a hand on his chest and speaks to him, though he doesn't respond.

There's a gap between the people watching. Then an aisle between seats. I can run now, stay low, dodge between them. She'll never find me in the darkness.

But I don't. Yet.

Because I'm curious too.

"Sir, can you hear me?" she repeats, while examining him for signs of injury.

He becomes calmer. That's when I notice, because I'm looking at him from the side, not the front like she is: there's blood trickling out of his ear.

"Gloria!" I shout, pointing, and then she sees it too. His ear seems to be moving. I know that's not normal. I once spent an hour looking in the mirror, trying to wiggle mine, after I saw it in a comedy. It doesn't work. The best I could do was shift the whole thing slightly by making extreme face contortions. When I read up on musculature articles after that, it confirmed what I suspected, that we don't have muscles throughout the ear: it's just cartilage. Once again, cartoons lie. So his ear isn't twitching because the man is moving it. That means something *else* is.

I step closer to see better. There is more blood now, and the man struggles again. He isn't trying to unclip the belt, it's more random, like he's having a fit and it hurts.

The blood runs down his neck and a spurt of it gushes out, splatting on the floor. Some of it goes on the upwards-shining lights, and instead of white those bits become red, lighting faces so that everyone seems blood-splashed. And something else is visible under his ear, little things sticking out through the hole in the middle, narrow pointed fingertips, or legs or something, hard and jittery.

Gloria doesn't use her fingers to examine the ear. She has left him, retreated to where I am.

The man stops twitching. Instead it's just those little wriggling limbs, coated in blood and stretching the ear hole as something tries to get out.

"Earworms," I say. I remember them from a horror-cast I saw once when Opal was out and I could watch things that were too old for me. "He's infested."

The other people who've been watching suddenly panic, and run, and some scream, and I don't know if it is fear or if they've caught the earworms too. Or maybe they overheard me. We don't hang around to see, or to watch what is coming out of the man's head and how big it really is, because Gloria has grabbed my hand and pulls me away ... except in the stampede someone treads on my foot – grown-up shoe crusher versus my five bare toes, not an even match – and it hurts so that I stumble and fall.

Gloria doesn't leave me. She doesn't even falter. She snatches me up as if I weigh nothing, like she's as strong as Bradden even without the obvious, big muscles; she holds me against her front,

up off the ground, safe; and she runs. I bounce up and down and
try to hold on, gripping around her neck, the bag in my clasped
hands jostling against her back.

If we weren't running it might be nice to be carried. Opal used
to put me on her shoulders before I got too big. Now it has to
just be piggy backs. Or, if she's being really nice, she crawls on
her hands and knees and I can ride her like a pony. But this rush
isn't too comfy, and there's a hard bulge under Gloria's cream
jacket, and I wonder if it is a lumpy boob, but then I realise
it's maybe a weapon, a gun. Like the one me and Opal found
amongst Daddy's private things when he died and we checked
his bedroom in case there was money.

My head is against Gloria's shoulder and I can smell her hair.
It doesn't smell like the shampoo I use at home, with the add-in
scents of fruits; hers smells more like chemicals (even though
everything is chemicals, really), and that's a bit sad, like maybe
Gloria doesn't have much fun with the little things in life. Maybe
she works too hard.

The ship being mostly in darkness means we can easily see the
little red glows around doors, and blue direction arrows embedded in walls and floors and ceilings. And, because I am looking
backwards over Gloria's shoulder, I see something else: another
of the big translucent cyan growths drifts through a wall into this
area. The new, larger tumour-clump glows brightly, the colour
rippling on the walls of this large room like lights on water,
though the ceilings are too high to reflect it back, that's just black
as if the roof has been cut off and it is night-time. Even with the
bouncing I notice a woman near the bluish-green mass fall over
and scream, and perhaps something else, like a darting line that

jabs out of the aquamarine cluster towards her head. Or maybe I imagined that. It's hard to tell when you're being jostled up and down, and we're amongst another group of panicking and screaming people, all shoving each other to escape the reclining seat chamber and down this narrow corridor that leads away, and when Gloria is knocked into the wall I release my bag from the impact, but Gloria keeps running.

"I need my bag, stop, I dropped it!" I yell, picturing it being trampled under feet in the gloomy shadows.

"Too many people, we need to get out of here," Gloria replies, not stopping. "Priorities, Clarissa. It's just toys and shoes."

I struggle to get down but it's no good, she's too strong, her arms are like metal even though she holds me without hurting me.

I don't care about the shoes. Glad they're gone. But it wasn't just toys. RearroBlox aren't *toys*. They're my way of talking to Bobo. I think he wanted me to talk to him again, to finish some process. It could have been important, but now he can't tell me. We can't make the shapes and patterns.

I stop squirming, stop reaching out as if I can pull the bag into my hand, and I let my arm fall down Gloria's back.

Bye bye, Bobo. I don't know when we can talk again.

Gloria leaves the main corridor for a quieter side passage. I recognise it from when the lights were on, near the private rooms. It leads to an exercise complex and gym. Muscle-meanie Agent Bradden had said he'd be going there a lot. But now people aren't wanting extra exercise: running to get somewhere safe probably counts as enough.

Once we're away from the yelling and shoving, Gloria plonks me down in a side seat and speaks into the Comm-Bond under her wrist skin.

"Bradden, where are you?"

His voice comes from the Comm-Bond's loudspeaker.

"Four decks down from our rooms. Went on a recce. Got intel that something bad's happening in the engine core. Maybe critical. I tried to ride the Spine, but without power the bullet cars have been disabled, can't traverse the zero-g vac tunnels at all, so I had to go on foot. Half the elevators have stopped working, people are panicking, the ship's lurching when AG has a fit, darkness causing accidents and tramplings – it's a fucking mess. I tried to contact you."

"I'm nearly at our room."

"Change of plan. We're getting off."

"Drop pods? Decelerate and fall out of Nullspace, or whatever this is?"

"I've gone one better, sorted out one of the VIP shuttles and a pilot. We can still velo-drop back to Realspace in the shuttle, and at least we'll have some flight control, and better protection than a civvie in a drop pod. They might as well be tissue paper in anything outside of minimal safety regs situations."

"Send me the route. We'll join you."

"We? I suppose that's still the mission. But if it becomes a burden, priority is self-extraction."

"Just hold the shuttle until I arrive!" She swipes the channel closed.

"We're getting off this ship, little one," Gloria says.

We. It's one of the good words. Opal uses it a lot. It is much warmer than the words grown-ups use more often, *I* and *you*.

I had been rubbing my toes. I don't think they got broken when they were squished, so we walk again. I hold Gloria's hand, the one that doesn't have the Comm-Bond under the skin. She glances at the screen regularly as it gives her a map of where we are, and where we should go, which doesn't always match up to the pale blue arrows which seem to float in the darkness, not attached to anything. These corridors are abandoned, meaning no shouting, no running feet, no screaming, nothing being knocked over.

I actually prefer exploring the ship by emergency radiance. The normal lights make things bright, reflective, harsh and distracting. But hushed darkness and soft glimmer are peaceful, as if I'm going to sleep in my bedroom, with Opal telling me a story by the faint glow of a subdued exterior skytower light. If I don't look up at Gloria's ghostly face, I can imagine it is Opal's hand I'm holding.

The ship lurches again, throwing us against a wall (lucky it wasn't a low-railed walkway balcony, or Gloria might have toppled over and squished). Neither of us is hurt. The bigger problem is that now even the emergency illuminations have gone out, and with no skywindows in this inner section there isn't even the blue-green cluster-cloud glow to show the way. It's like having your eyes closed *and* having thick eyelids, so that there's no light passing through to show the blood swooshes.

Almost immediately, the place brightens again. But this time it's Gloria holding out her hand, and white light shines from the palm.

"Sweet," I say. "You can't lose things if they're under your skin."

"There are mandatory upgrades in my role, including ocular or palm-implanted recording devices. I didn't fancy having my eyes removed."

"Urgh, me neither. Squishy. And it hurts even if I just poke myself in the eye."

We continue down the dark corridor. The beam from her palm creates sliding shadows to each side, as if they keep retreating behind objects as we approach.

"Do you do that often?" she asks.

"Yes. It's the best thing to do after eating a pizza."

"I prefer to poke myself in the eye after eating chips."

We reach a bank of elevators, but they are all dark.

"Oh no, after *chips* you should always poke someone *else* in the eye," I tell her. "That's much more polite."

Gloria tries the buttons on the elevators anyway. She'd said we needed to go down another few decks.

The floor is getting hotter. There's no carpet on this passage-way.

"How do you learn to talk like you?" I ask.

"What do you mean?"

"All poshy-accent, like a newscaster."

Gloria is feeling around the wall next to the elevators.

"I don't have an accent," she says. It doesn't sound like she's trying to trick me, not irony on purpose, even though the precise way she says the *-ent* is totally different from the way me and Opal say it. Gloria says each letter, and the *e* is like in *peg*. We would say it like one of the *uhs* in *burger*, and not bother with the *t* at the end.

"You do," I insist. "I can hear it."

"It's just the way we talk on my world."

"What planet is that?"

"Rosarium Prime."

"I don't know much about that one."

"That's because there isn't much *to* know."

Gloria has found some kind of catch, and a big wall panel creaks open towards us, on hinges. As it does, some of the air is sucked into that new area. Gloria leans in, shines her palm light. It's a narrow shaft with a ladder going up and down.

"Emergency access," she says.

"I wasn't born on Mossareid," I reply.

"I know. I read your files."

"Fressus was nicer. Instead of skytowers blocking the view, you could see across the water, watch the sun making a golden-green path to the edge of the sky. Plus: no crawly Decapede migrations each second summer."

"Talking of crawlies, we need to climb down the ladder," she says.

"Oopsie. It's deep."

"It'll be fine."

"It'll be a squishy mess if we slip."

"I'm going to carry you."

"It will be harder on a ladder."

"I'm stronger than you think." Maybe I don't seem convinced, because she squats next to me. "As well as subcutaneous implants, Agents have reinforced skeletons, some hormone dispersal and regulation systems, muscular enhancements, and low-grade military mods. I could pick you up and run with you for hours. I will *not* drop you. That's a promise."

"Circle your heart and hope to pop?"

Gloria draws a circle on her chest.

Bedroom Decapede

TURQUOISE AND RED

Gloria doesn't want to risk me on her back, in case I can't hold on tight enough and fall, so picks me up at her front. I wrap my arms around her neck, and legs around her waist, with my face against her ear and hair. Her hair isn't just a lighter colour than mine, it's smoother, doesn't seem so tangly. Kind of like she controls it, can't have anything out of place or she'll get the sack. That reminds me of all the operations she had, just to get this job. I bet some of them really hurt. It would make much more sense to get a job as a storyteller or something, making films and books. Instead of painful operations I could just lie on my bed and eat nice food and stroke a doggy, or even have two doggies, and just make things up out of my dreams or whatever. It would be easy, and people would pay me millions of creds and want to put me on the cover of ent-casts and animation-mags.

Once she's sure I am safely clinging on, she swings out over the cold emptiness and grips the rungs tight. I can tell it's awkward for her having me on her front, meaning she has to lean out further from the ladder to make space for me as she descends. It will be more tiring. But, this way, if I slip, she could catch me, or push close to the ladder to squash me in place.

Her heartbeats are strong. I can feel them against my chest from her boobs. I don't have boobs yet, but Opal has started to get them. I think it annoys her, because she's worried it will make climbing up balconies harder or something like that. When I see her again I will tell her not to worry, because even though Gloria's are bigger (but not silly big like some vid-stars, not like melons; these are more like lemons, which is a similar word but makes rubbish Fizz, even MelonFizz is better, and that's quite rubbish too), Gloria can still climb without them getting caught on her arms, and she can still run fast. So that's all good.

It's hard to see much as we descend this shaft with cool, stale-smelling air blowing up past us. The white palm light is still on, but most of the time she's using her hand to climb so the shaft keeps going dark as she grips the next rung.

Thud thud thud as she descends, regular, untiring. I hope her shoes have good grips, otherwise she'll regret not going barefoot like me.

I stay as still as I can. That's my way of helping. And I talk to her as we climb down, without expecting her to answer because she is busy. I talk about Opal, and about the different seasons on Mossareid, and my favourite ent-casts – usually animal ones – and what we eat. I do *not* talk about Opal stealing food for us, or trying to hack the grid so we get free power, nor the gun we found in our parents' things. I don't want to get Opal into trouble. If I'm really good, and if Opal manages not to fight too many people, and doesn't punch any more security guards, maybe they'll realise it was a mistake to split us up, and I won't need to go to Corporate Academy, and Opal won't need to be in the army (especially as it seems daft to give her a job that makes her *more* dangerous if they are worried about her being naughty), and they'll let us go home again as long as we sign a long piece of paper that says we agree to be good. Hopefully we won't have to sign it in blood, because *urgh*.

With each heavy footstep her shoes clunk on the metal ladder rungs, and it echoes up and down the shaft.

Opal could sign it for me, in that case. I bet she would. She's a good big sister like that, and she isn't bothered when she gets cuts or bruises. She's a lot tougher than some of the boys from our skytower.

My eyes were closed while talking, but then I open them and I can see more than just from Gloria's palm light. The shaft is faintly ripply and turquoise, as if deep underwater, with a faraway light shining down. Gloria's so focussed on the ladder rungs, where palm light spills out with every stepped descent, that she hasn't noticed yet.

Above us, edging through the shaft walls at an angle that brings it down towards us, is one of the bulbous clusters.

I tap her shoulder and point up. She sees, then descends even faster.

"Argh, we just passed an exit, can't risk going back up, near that *thing*. Hold on tight, this will be bumpy."

And it *is* bumpy. When I try to talk my voice shakes from Gloria's rapid climbing.

"I don't think it's intentionally following us," I say. "When I looked out of a porthole at the clusters, they were hardly shifting against the clouds: it was *us* that moved. This big spaceship, I mean. The cluster things were all connected together by strands. The clouds stay outside, but these clustery clumps and strands don't seem solid, not like the ship, so as we move we pass through them. Or they pass through us. Like different wavelengths of radiation penetrate different materials. Did you know, even the visual wavelengths of light can get through a certain amount of soft tissue, like your eyelids? So they aren't chasing: it's us, we're invading their home."

"That would make me feel better if it wasn't getting closer while we're stuck in a shaft."

"And I don't think we can risk being near it," I say, remembering the jabbing needle that streaked out of one, so fast it was only a blink, towards a woman when we were running, and maybe also towards that man's head when he was strapped in the chair. "Something bad happens."

Gloria's foot slips, and we dangle for a second by her hands before she finds a grip and continues. I always said shoes were evil. She's muttering under her breath, some of it bad words.

"I'm not scared," I whisper in her ear. "And you don't need to be, either."

She does a deep nose breath, a long exhale, while still bumpily descending, then says, "Check."

I keep watching upwards while Gloria just concentrates on climbing down. The blue bulbous lumps drift towards us faster than Gloria can descend. It's a big cluster, too, now filling the shaft and extending beyond it through the walls. It's hard to judge distance but maybe that's only twice the length of my Mossareid home with Opal, so what's that, twenty metres away? And what is the reach of the jabbing lines? About that? Do the bigger ones have an even further reach? There's no point saying anything, because I can tell if Gloria tries to go any faster we'll probably just end up falling.

Sometimes you have to accept that the universe isn't perfect, and there's not much you can do about it if you're just one itty bitty person. Opal said that. Or something like it.

I wish she was here now.

She's *really* good at climbing.

"This is it!" says Gloria. "The ledge that means we're at the next floor. Thank the Purities!"

It's not much of a ledge. The greenish blue light from above (worryingly bright now) shows it to be hardly wider than someone's foot. Gloria stays on the ladder and leans out, looking for the catch.

There's another tremor throughout the ship, and moaning from down the shaft. Could be metal bending, or monsters hurting: they'd sound about the same. I can tell Gloria is struggling; she slips and has to put her toe on that tiny, perforated metal grille for balance, though if there's a bigger vibration it might shake her leg right off, maybe the one hand on the rungs won't be enough, and we'll tumble. Away from the cluster, yay; towards the splatty floor, boo.

There's a click, and a change in pressure and air motion, and the sound changes too, and Gloria swings us through the gap onto solid ground, but she doesn't put me down. She runs along this dark corridor, then looks back when we've gone far enough, and we see the edges of the cluster through the wall, sliding down, weird strings running off to other places, maybe joining to lumpy gatherings on other floors. That's a useful thing to remember, that the strands could act as early warnings, especially when there's no windows. Last thing you'd want is a cluster to suddenly appear under your feet from the floor below, or through the wall right next to you in a narrow corridor.

And then it's passed, and the cobalt blue fades, and we just have the white light from Gloria's palm.

"You okay?" she asks, lowering me to the floor. It is probably as much a relief for her as it is for me.

"Check." I'm already getting better at speaking like her.

Gloria examines her wrist map and leads me on.

"Thanks for carrying me," I say.

"You're welcome. I'm just glad you're ten, not twelve. That extra ten kilos might have been a struggle."

The main lights flicker and come back on again as we walk, and we have to squint to adjust to the brightness as the light glares from all the white surfaces of this bare passageway that looks dirty and unused. Then there's a crackling sound on the loudspeakers, a broken *bing bing bing bing*, a whisper of scratchy voice, hissing like static, other noises, and amongst all that there are screams, really horrible ones, and more bings, then the ship lurches hard and the sound fades out and the lights die again.

Gloria squeezes my hand.

"I can't get younger, but I could go on a diet so I'm lighter," I tell her, because I don't think either of us wants to talk about the screaming.

"Any lighter and there'd be nothing to you. Maybe it's good that you like eating pots of choc spread."

"Bones would weigh the same. I read that they're about twelve per cent of body weight."

"Mine are more, twenty-five per cent, so that I weigh seventy-five kilograms. Level one reinforced skeletal structures do nothing for a woman's self-esteem during biossessments."

We're heading back through the outer bit of the ship, where the shuttles will be. Small windows line this passage again, rippling the walls in aqua. We stop for a moment and look out at the rolling, foggy clouds, wondering how far it extends.

I realise I don't want to slip away any more. Gloria's proved that I'm safer with her than running around on my own. That's what I'll tell Opal if she asks, anyway. Opal would find that easier to believe than me saying Gloria seems like a friend.

The peace is interrupted by a booming sound, like a huge drum.

"Gunfire," Gloria explains, moving quickly, so that I have to do extra half steps to keep up. "We're nearly there!"

We go up a curved passage, and then it opens out into something that looks more like a warehouse. There are reinforced storage boxes of different sizes secured here. We hadn't seen or heard people for a while, but we see and hear them *now*, an angry crowd ahead of us, blocking the view of whatever they're facing and shouting at, all vaguely illuminated in red flashing warning lights. The room slopes downwards in half-circles, like an old structure called an amphitheatre. There is a super-grip rubberised floor on the walkway, and the raised textures of it tickle my feet.

Gloria carries me so that I don't get my toes squished again as she pushes through the angry and scared people (and it's not easy to tell which are which, so maybe they're the same thing really). There's a clear space beyond them, sloping downwards to Agent

Bradden, who holds a stubby pistol, pointing it towards the crowds, keeping them back. Behind him is an open hatch from which the flashing red light spills out, stark and low, illuminating the scene. The shadows cast onto walls make people look huge and gangly as if they dance around a fire.

"Why have you got guns?" I ask Gloria.

"To protect you, Clarissa. In case anyone tries to hurt or kidnap you."

The bouncing as she runs down the steps and then elbows her way through the crowd stops me from asking more questions.

When Agent Bradden sees us, he says, "Took your damn time!"

People seem madder as we approach him, surging forward with a push, and he shouts at them, and points his gun again, telling them to stay back.

"Pilot's running system checks, but the shuttle only seats twelve," he says.

I don't know how many people are trying to get aboard, and begging, and calling names, but it is more than twelve. More than two lots of twelve. Maybe even more than three.

And beyond them, as I look over Gloria's shoulder, I can see something no one else can, because the crowd is facing us.

Some of the cyan strands are moving through the wall and thickening, as if we're drifting into another band of the bluish-green cancer growths, and it's happening pretty fast.

"We can only take some of you," Gloria shouts. "Women and children, step forward."

Someone notices the teal cluster approaching from behind, drifting surely towards the group. And towards us. And the shuttle. That starts the screaming again, and suddenly it's like a riot as the crowd heaves towards us. A woman with her hair shaved into lines is knocked over and trampled; a strong man in a vest top yells and shoves people out of the way; a person with a beard and metallic arm is trying to drag someone to the front.

Gloria runs on board with me, through the red-flashing airlock, away from the yells and the panicked screams and the gunshots, which must be Agent Bradden firing into the air, or at the crowd; and then the door slides shut with a thump, hiding the view of people falling, possibly shot, possibly getting jabbed by that cluster which is still moving towards us. Agent Bradden is sweating and yelling to the pilot to go, to go *now*, and the craft vibrates as torsion drives fire up.

A central aisle is lined by two seats on each side, in three rows, and a window next to each outer seat. At the front an open door leads to the area for the pilot, toilets and storage. The soft lighting isn't enough to compete with the vivid aquamarine outside, which ripples through the windows.

A floor-shuddering clunk reverberates as we detach from the Solace, and then we streak away. But the view outside isn't steady, and the shuttle's floor isn't either.

"I can't get control," shouts the pilot.

The transport tumbles but the artificial gravity is working overtime, so we're able to move by holding on to the backs of seats, even though the view outside is spinning, spinning. Sometimes the Solace we've just left moves across the view, a huge whale of a ship, though we're already so far away from the release jets that I can't make out where we launched from, and I'm glad of that, because I'd then imagine all the people on the other side of the hatch, and what was happening to them, and if I saw the cluster floating out through the hull of the Solace I'd know it was bad.

And it still is, for us, too. Throughout the clouds are huge numbers of interconnected growths, strands stretching like spider webs between them, and although they're far apart we could easily tumble into and through one super-quick, and it might all be over for us then.

"We're screwed, absolutely fucking screwed," says Agent Bradden, and he looks sweaty and shaky.

"Calm down," Gloria tells him, in a soft voice. "Activate your hormonal regulators."

"I can't. Diagnostics show a breakdown in my endocrine systems. It's been on the edge for a while. They were going to take the opportunity to replace it during my next op, hopefully something more reliable. They never treat us to top stuff! Just faulty military leftovers, they don't respect us and our role, Gloria, they just think of us as low rankers, to get the job done. I might as well look different, I may as well be a low life, this isn't what I signed on for! This –"

"Bradden, hand me your firearm."

He's been waving it around as he shouts, whereas Gloria is calm, moving slowly to be within arm's reach of him.

"I'll look after it for you," she adds. "Protocol RA12."

And he nearly does hand it over. Beads of sweat trickle down his face. Then he pulls his arm back, and slides the gun into a holster under his cream jacket – a jacket which now has lots of dirty marks on it.

"No," he says. "I'm under control. And these are dangerous circumstances. I might need it."

Another judder in the shuttle throws us to the side, nearly spilling us onto the seats.

"What the fuck?" Agent Bradden shouts.

We head to the front, gripping headrests each time it feels like the floor is sliding, and it might look funny, as if we're climbing a steep hill, because that's what the artificial gravity simulates at the moment. But there are twelve seats with no one sitting on them. There are four of us on the shuttle. Many people were left behind. Left behind to die.

I wish we'd let them all in. It would have been a squishy squeeze, like feet-in-face and adults-sat-on-each-others-knees kind of squeeze, but maybe we'd have all got in and away.

No one asked me what I wanted to do.

Grown-ups always decide for themselves and just do it.

I think there wouldn't be so many people killing and dying if kids were given a say in it.

In the cockpit area the glowing displays are holographically projected from the smart panel, along with key controls, and there are some physical manipulators, too. I recognise sensor, comms and flight control systems; the rest are a mystery.

"This is a nightmare!" says the pilot, who wears a uniform in the design of other Solace crew, though this uniform includes a hat. "We should be in void but we're not; yet it isn't behaving like atmospherics, either. Control's partial, we've not even resolved the spin yet. It's as if what we see doesn't correspond to what the sensors detect, or what's actually out there. On top of which, the systems can't decide what way is up, leading to mismatches between AG and propulsion, which I have to keep resetting; and I'm picking up nothing from the IPS."

"Which means?" asks Gloria.

"IPS, Interstellar Positioning System. But there are no Passive Transmit Beacons out there. We're definitely not in UFS space."

Many of the radiant screens show errors, and spinning geometries that are probably not meant to be spinning. At least we get a good view of the outside, because nearly all the front of the shuttle is transparent. Huge, curved panels give a panoramic view, as if there isn't really anything separating us from what we see. Clouds pulse, sometimes seeming to suck in and then expand when they overlap, glowing like blue-green fire inside and even more brightly at the edges; and amongst that are the turquoise groups of papery, attached globes, almost like giant wasps' nests connected by strands. A few times we spin just out of range of one of them as the pilot moves fast, activating thrusters and boosting jets, and recalibrating screens.

Agent Bradden splutters suggestions while gripping the pilot's headrest, asking if the pilot's tried this, or that, until the pilot snaps: "If you can do better then take over! I'd really love it if you did. If not, then get back to the seats and stop interfering!"

Agent Bradden starts arguing with him, and they both shout and ignore Gloria telling them to concentrate, and I just want to cover my eyes and ears (which would need an extra hand) but in the spins I think I see one of the clusters flashing past, and each time we rotate it looks nearer.

Maybe Gloria notices too, because she kneels and hugs me, and now everyone's seen it and yells in a different way.

"Look out, that's too close to port side –"

"Pulling back and ejecting mass –"

"It's on the other side now because we're fucking spinning!"

And then one voice cuts out and I sense a flash of cobalt blue, a jabbing line, and the pilot is still in his seat, strapped there just like the man on the Solace, shaking. He's dribbling and making a kind of eager wheezing sound that's really high-pitched for a man, more like what an excited doggy might do.

It doesn't sound so nice when a man is doing it.

His eyes stare all around, looking at one thing and another, something, everything, though I don't think he's really seeing anything at all.

"Oh fuck," says Agent Bradden. He draws his gun and pushes it against the wheezing pilot's head.

"Maybe it's not what we think!" says Gloria. "Perhaps he had a pre-existing condition. It's a fit of some kind, or ..." But she peters out, because it doesn't sound like she's even convincing herself. "How come it's just him affected?"

"We only just clipped that – *whatever it is* – out there," says Bradden. "Not too close, but obviously close enough. Maybe it only affects one person, whoever's nearest?"

"Maybe your reinforced bones helped," I say. "Block whatever it is that jabs out."

But Agent Bradden speaks to Gloria, not me. "You told it? That's a breach."

"She's smart. It's obvious we're not Societal Services agents. They don't get military upgrades."

"Now who's breaking protocol?" He lowers the weapon, but it is held loosely, not pointing anywhere specific. "And if we were protected by our obviously thick skulls, that led us into this stupid situation, what's protecting *her*? Maybe we should make sure anyone without a thick skull doesn't cause us problems."

"Don't do this," says Gloria.

And then I see blood, and the popping sound isn't the gun, it's the ear of the pilot which kind of blows out this time, not a slow crawl out like before. Maybe the conditions here are different. Gore spatters on the clear cockpit glass, spurts on Agent Bradden's hand and face, and that cream suit gets a splash of bright crimson. He winces, staggers back but there's no room, he falls into the empty copilot seat. Something sort of jumps or fast-stretches from the pilot's torn-open ear hole, something nearly as big as my hand, leaving strands of tissue which flap down the dead pilot's neck, and I can even see into that hole for a second. There are all sorts of colours inside a skull, not just reds but yellows and greys too. It's so icky because the grey might be that horrible type of jelly, the one only monsters would eat at a Reset Day party: brain jelly.

Agent Bradden lifts his feet off the floor, trying to locate the thing, but the bloody smears stop soon after where it landed. Gloria picks me up and backs out of the cockpit.

"You intervened," Agent Bradden shouts. "If you'd let me empty his head we'd have killed it! Now it could be anywhere!"

"It's not gone past me." Gloria is now back in the main aisle of the shuttle and puts me down. "Clarissa, you wait out here. It must be under the controls. We'll find it."

And she hits the panel to close the door so that it slides silently down, closing her in with Agent Bradden and the ear worm or whatever it is, and I don't know which one of those is worse.

The world outside spins. Greenish blue ripples across everything. I feel sick. Properly sick. I wish Opal was here. She'd know what to do. She'd tell me to run. And if I couldn't run, to hide.

I crawl under a double seat. It's low, the gap is small, but I fit. I can often find a way to fit. The seat presses against my back, and the floor against my chest, and I use my toes and feet to wiggle back further. Although it is like being squished it actually makes it less nauseating because I can't see out of the windows from here, even though the cyan still washes back and forth over everything like a wave of electric. Bright and dark and darker yet, then bright again, back and forth and –

It's on the floor in front of me, only half a metre from my face. Somehow it moved when the bright aqua glow passed. It seemed to lift out of the floor but that's an illusion, maybe. Perhaps it's just really *really* fast.

Agent Bradden and Gloria are talking in the cockpit, searching, opening access panels, checking equipment and storage, even though *it's already here.*

Looking at me.

Well, it doesn't have eyes, so maybe not looking, as such.

It's the size of my palm, browny-purple but with reddy bits that might be from inside the pilot's head. It isn't a shape of creature I've ever seen before. It definitely has things that might be legs or feelers, but they are bent back or jointed in a way that means I can't work out which way they move, or really how long they are. Up close, and still, maybe some of them are different, longer limbs, sort of scratchy-looking, with fine hairs on them. The way the legs fold back hides the head and body mostly, but what I do see seems super thin, so maybe the leggy-feely bits *are* the body, or a head, or a long neck. It might have no eyes – or maybe the sticky-out bits are eyes? – but I still think it is assessing me. It sort of twitches, a ripple moving from limb to limb, then it settles lower.

"What are you?" I whisper, making sure my head is turned so my breath doesn't go straight onto it, in case mouth-breathing is like a swear word for creatures and it attacks, or in case it sees down into my throat and decides that looks like a nice warm place to make a nest.

It doesn't answer or move.

Well, my head hasn't exploded, that's good so far, but I can't risk shouting for Gloria because that might startle it. Startled or frightened things are unpredictable and dangerous. Ponies, Agent Braddens, big sisters, spindly things that crawl out of ears and brains.

"How do you get into heads? I read about anatomy quite recently, in a Cyclopedia, and our brains are held in membranes, and I remember the three layers by the acronym D-A-P, like Doggies Are People – Dura Mater, Arachnoid, Pia Mater – and the cerebrospinal fluid which protects our brains is in the sub-arachnoid space, which is like another word for spiders, even though you're not a spider, but did you get confused? Do you know about those layers and the tiny cavities there?"

It sort of flows to the side, that ripple of limbs again, but I think it listens, or tries to.

"Do you even realise we're people, and that you tunnelling into our brains kills us? I wish you could talk about it."

In a way, it reminds me of Bobo, because it is small, like him. I have to talk to Bobo with my thoughts, not my lips, and maybe that's the same for this little thing?

I open my mind and close my eyes, because that way the black is like a canvas for pictures to appear on with no distractions. And the second I do it I feel something I can't explain, maybe it's fear from somewhere outside me. So I keep my eyes closed and I talk to it again out loud, but this time I try to think the words at it too, so it isn't just sounds but is me kind of reaching out, like sending a vid message, and I am not sure if I imagine it or if it's real details but I can almost picture the inside of a blue-green cluster, like eggs; no, tiny chambers; no, it's a *nursery*.

"You're only young, aren't you?" I say, lips and mind. "Like me. And you're scared. You didn't want to leave. And you didn't mean to hurt anyone. I understand that. My mummy died while I was being born, and I was made an orphan. I don't remember it, I was a baby, like you, but Opal told me. And years later I got a new mummy and daddy, they adopted us and they eventually died too, but that's not the point: it's the first mummy I am thinking of, my blood mummy who died giving birth to me, because that wasn't my fault even though I'm sad about it every day. It's just how the universe is. That's what Opal says. It's not fair. It hurts. Maybe you're sorry, too."

And then it's blank, the connection gone, replaced with a brief sting behind my eyes, like they've been pinged with elastic; and when I open them I don't see *the thing*, I see a big black shoe, where the heel grinds left and right, the sole of it crushing something against the floor, something that squidges out from under it in pasty crunches.

Agent Bradden's shoe.

"Whoo-hee, got the abomination!" he says.

I hadn't noticed that him and Gloria had stopped talking, hadn't heard the cockpit door slide open, hadn't seen his shadow in the shifting teal lights. I was so focussed on the scared little thing, and now it was *dead*.

I crawl out and bite his leg, hard as I can, the rough brush of his trouser material against my lips. I don't manage to bite deep, maybe not even breaking skin before he kicks out, shakes me off, but I hate him, I hate him for that squished smudge on the grippy carpet.

"You little weirdo!" he says, rubbing his ankle and glaring at me from a face still speckled with icky blood splats. "I save your life and that's your thanks? I should have let you die. Your sort don't deserve to live with us."

Gloria pushes past him, kneels next to me, giving me a hug, while Agent Bradden stomps into the cockpit, muttering something, then yells "Fuck!" Gloria leads me to the cockpit too, to see what the problem is *now*. I carefully skirt around the sad little pile of the alien thing.

The wide view of the aquamarine storm spinning all around us is the same as before, but something is happening to the clusters, and the strands connecting them. The filaments get brighter and contract, almost like they're angry, pulling in, so the clusters move closer and closer together, tighter packed. Instead of it looking like we're tumbling through a sparse minefield, it now looks like we're going to be tumbling into a tight net.

"It's the same all around," he says, unclipping the pilot and tipping his body to the floor so Agent Bradden can take the main controls. "And the E-Spac Collision Avoidance System still can't detect – or evade – them." He wipes the blood-spattered glass with his sleeve, which just smears it, then deals with the warnings being displayed. The way he operates the systems shows that he is trained to fly a shuttle. Even if Gloria *hadn't* told me, by now I'd have realised they weren't normal agents. Were they mysterious UFS Wardens?

"Take the damn copilot seat," he shouts at Gloria. "We've got to gain control, somehow get through the gaps before they shrink too much, otherwise we're going into a mass of those nest things and we're *all* going to get an earful."

Gloria lets go of my hand, strapping into the other seat, activating manual controls and running diagnostics.

"Go to a seat at the back, make sure you fasten the seatbelt," she tells me, half her attention on what she's doing with a display about gyroscopic counterbalances.

I'm glad to get out of that gruesome cockpit. You can smell the stuff that spurted from the pilot's head, and it's horrible, sort of makes you choke. I sidestep the smear that was maybe going to be a friend, and despite the rolling – which is even more irregular now as they fight to get some kind of control to the shuttle – I make it into a seat and clip the belt across my waist, tightening it so that it's right for a kid.

I'm on my own.

I close my eyes tight. I try calling out to Opal again, as much of a scream as I can in my head, but it just echoes back, like she's nowhere, or I'm nowhere, and that far away echo makes me lonelier than ever, like the connection to the little dead thing that's now an emptiness too.

I try reaching out to the clusters instead. Blue-green light washes over my eyelids, and some of that gets through to create flowing swoosh patterns, and that makes it easier to picture the nests or whatever they are outside. But I can't talk to them. Can't feel them. Maybe they're shells. Maybe they're angry. I just picture them closing in, to trap us, to stab at us.

"I'm here," says a quiet and scratchy voice.

"Bobo?" I don't say anything out loud, just answer with thoughts.

"It's me," he adds. His voice is fainter than before, and still has that funny edge to it that never happened in the past.

"How can you talk to me if I don't have my RearroBlox?"

"Let's just say this is a special place. And I'm always with you anyway, somewhere deep inside. I have to tell you that you're going to die, very soon, unless you let me help."

There are more shapes behind my eyelids now, that remind me of the different-sided geometrics I had to learn for a test once, but these are moving, and somehow all connected to each other so one edge on a shape is also a border on a neighbouring figure, all shared.

And I think I can see bits of Bobo in those shapes, often just at the edge, so that when I focus on an area the fur fades into a line, and the eyes become a vertex, eyes that are still the wrong colours, swirly colours. Maybe the contours are like cage bars, and he's trapped, just like our shuttle is stuck within this turquoise space.

In another part of my mind I can hear Agent Bradden and Gloria shouting and swearing at the controls, at space, at each other, but I tune that out so it is just deeper blackness, just me and Bobo and the patterns.

"The images I'm showing you, it's a kind of key," Bobo says, "a way of opening a tunnel down here. It's something I could teach you, because your brain has the desired prerequisites for ... has been shaped simultaneously for exit parameters ... woof! Sorry, no, it's a magic doorway."

His voice keeps changing, the scratchiness sort of fading away and then coming back, like he is moving nearer and further as we spin, or like he is practising different voices for a joke.

"Will it open a door to get away so we won't die?"

"Yes! Woof! But there is so little time, I can't train you. Not now. But later, maybe. I don't want you to die, Clarissa. And you don't want Gloria to die, I think? Woof! You can save her. You just have to trust me."

"How?"

"You have to go deeper into the black in your mind, which is like sleep, like – comatose reductionism, flatline of activity, electrical, pulse – woof! Like a nice little rest. I'm your ever-friend, your always-friend, you can trust me! It's too complex for you, but I can do it if you relinquish cardiovascular and conscious reflex – control – let me help my friend! I need a physical organic presence to unlock the space between Topias, to make the connection – to get you to a safer place. A party place, woof! You have to let me take over. Now. Let me put you in my box for a while. We swap places, I save you."

The voice is scratchy again. The shapes glow so bright now, and I am falling, even though it is just alterations in AG maybe, like going into a black hole in my head, so that even Bobo echoes now, and I don't like his voice again as it repeats, like I'm moving faster and faster away from everything, so far away.

"Will you give me my body back?" I ask.

"Of course. Doggy circles its heart. Woof! Now you just need to sink into your ickle bickle head."

And so I think about Opal, and the time when my second mummy and daddy died, the ones I actually remember, and me and Opal were left alone in the apartment, trying to be secret, and I cried in bed while Opal hugged and rocked me.

"Did they die because of me, like what happened with my first mummy?" I asked.

"No. None of it was your fault."

"But now things won't ever be good again, will they?"

"Of course they will. Our world has changed but we're only a part of the world, and the rest goes on," she explained. "Close your eyes. Think about when we were on Fressus and you were small and I took you to the city's edge and we walked along the artificial sandy area that they called the beach, while the others slept. Do you remember that?"

I nodded, because I did remember, and dreamt of it sometimes.

"Try and remember the wet sand beneath your feet, and the cool edge of the water when a wave washed up to our ankles."

And suddenly I *could* feel it. The peacefulness of the place, so early in the morning that it was just us out and about, the only noises were the crunch of sand and the lapping water. A cool breeze blew in from the endless ocean, refreshing my cheeks, and the warming morning sun shone down from the clear bluish sky. The air had that spicy-of-sea salty tang, and we stayed away from the edge where it dropped off into deep, *deep* water. Opal held my hand tight to make sure I couldn't go near it, because of the

big fishes, and I liked her hand closing over mine, because she
was protecting me.

And I remember that memory of a memory now as I sink into
my head. So much has changed but the world goes on, and if
we were on Fressus now, at that beach, at dawn, it would be the
same. It is only us that have changed, not the real world.

And I fall further and then I hit the bottom and it's hard,
knocks me out, even the shapes are gone –

FREDDIE BOBO

YELLOW AND PURPLE

"Clarissa, are you all right?"

Gloria's voice. My eyes open and the blackness fades away. There's no cyan, either. Instead everything's glowing in a harsh yellow light, which seems weird after the other colour had dominated for so long. That change would be a relief if the yellow wasn't so bright it hurt, and – somehow, that makes no sense – a yellow that felt *cold* in my head. It's the colour of a hard-skinned bitter lemfruit Opal stole once, where we didn't know what to do with it, so we cut it and ate the face-scrunching sourness. This isn't the gold of warmth, it's the lemon of a burning acid sun trapped in a dead freezer.

We no longer seem to be tumbling, but instead diving down, so that Gloria grips my seat, and the straps cut tight into me as I lean forward.

"We got gravity, Lefos!" Agent Bradden shouts from the cockpit. "No idea what happened, and can't see for shit in this yellow icy layer – minus two sixty degrees C – but at least some of the systems are functional now."

My mouth is dry. "I think so," I croak, and she squeezes my hand.

The clouds outside don't swirl like the cyan ones had. This is more like looking into a spotlight so blinding that you can't see the shape controlling it. I touch the glass but pull my hand back quickly. Icy. In fact, the cabin is already chilling, and our breath forms dragon mist when we breathe out.

I shiver, and Gloria puts her strong arm around my shoulders, unclipping me from the seat, and leading me towards the cockpit.

"Any hope?" Gloria asks Agent Bradden.

The pilot's body has rolled against one of the lower curved view windows. The blood from his head hole is darker in places where it trickled down his neck, sort of crusty. The cockpit smells like a butcher's outlet in a mega-market.

"Still no Passive Transmit Beacons, so location remains unknown," he says, struggling to keep the shuttle's nose up. "However, the scanners have detected land – well, an apparent centre of mass – nineteen kilometres below us. We must have decelerated enough to drop out of Nullspace, and somehow reappeared in a Realspace planetary orbit. That's lucky, even though we're falling – hopefully there will be trace atmosphere lower down and we can transition to flight mode. I've sent out SID signals on all frequencies. No response yet."

SID. Ship In Distress. An appropriate signal when the engines emit high-pitched whining like they're in pain.

Then the craft shudders and the engine noise goes quieter and red lights start flashing in the cockpit.

"One of the torsion drives has failed. Frozen up," he says.

Gloria climbs into the copilot chair and straps in, because now we are plummeting nose first again. We can't see anything different in the yellow blinding vista that fills the panorama ahead of us, but the dip pushes us towards that cold glass. I grip onto the back of Gloria's chair and watch. She's trying to readjust the AG systems and run diagnostics on the frozen engine, while Agent Bradden boosts the other two motors and raises the nose with expulsion jets. One of the cutaway screens shows a side-view holographic of the shuttle, and how the main torsion drive outlets had been rotated to face down, but have frozen solid so only secondary jets and movable fins are available to control angle of descent.

A second torsion drive freezes up and ceases with yet more alarms, louder now, and we roll to the side. Gloria silences the alarms and redirects the limited thermal stores to the torsion drives to try and bring them up to operational levels. Agent Bradden is controlling descent and rotation with anything that still works.

Then the foggy yellow disappears. We're falling out of it, as if it's a cloud layer, and as we drop away the view is replaced with a purple landscape below, which seems mostly flat and barren, like an amethyst desert.

"Height seventeen kilometres," he says. "Unless we get the torsion drives back online for thrust, we'll hit the ground in under two minutes."

"Already warming up." Gloria is sliding bars on her display up to higher levels. "Atmos?"

"We got trace at this level, with hardly any drag or turbulence," he replies. "Deformable wings now active, so if we can restart the torsion drives we'll have enough lift to regain control."

We're already more level. Now it's as if we're falling sideways towards the land, and the AG cancels some of the sensation so that it's just a slight pull to our right. But we're definitely dropping. Fast. The hull vibrates from the atmosphere outside streaking past us. The frozen yellow cloud lights are already further away, and the purplish ground nearer.

It would be supermax bad if we got here and still ended up all squashed and dead.

"I can ask for help," I say, quietly.

"Don't distract us," snaps Agent Bradden.

I ignore him. "It was me that got us out of the turquoise cloud space," I tell Gloria. "I have a friend who talks to me in my head. I gave him control for a while and he did something, like unlocking, and he said he'd take us to another thing called a Topia, and when I woke up we were here. We don't have to get splatted."

Gloria gets out of her chair and kneels down next to me. "It was just coincidence, Clarissa. You were knocked out by the stress and extreme conditions."

"No! He did it. I could ask him again and see if he can put us somewhere safer. It's worth a try," I say.

That's when I notice Agent Bradden has stood up too, and he's pointing his gun towards Gloria's head.

Correction, *my* head.

The black hole where bullets or whatever come out seems pretty big when I look into it.

Gloria must detect something is wrong, because she glances up, sees Agent Bradden, and immediately rises in front of me at the same time as gliding a hand under her jacket and drawing her own grey pistol. It's a really smooth movement. No snags, no fumbles. I bet she practices.

"Move out of the way," says Agent Bradden. The craft's frame rattles and judders so much I worry he could fire by accident.

"Put the weapon down," says Gloria.

He sounds sort of shaky in his voice, but Gloria speaks firmly, like a teacher when someone's in trouble.

"It's all her," he says. "I knew it! When she talked to that thing that came out of his head." He tilts his neck towards the pilot's body, but doesn't wave his gun hand or look away.

"Think about this," says Gloria. "We're going to die unless we work together."

"The backwards freak made us face all that stuff, or attracted it like a magnet for weirdness, who knows? She's more dangerous than the cretin she appears to be. Can't you see? You're not blind, Lefos. She's not *really* a girl. The labs, yeah? Get your fucking gun out of my face and move aside."

The ground is definitely getting nearer. I also notice green lights appearing on the console. That's normally a good thing. Except the gun pointing is keeping them too busy to do anything about it, and I don't want to try myself in case I press the wrong button. Or, more likely, Agent Bradden shoots me and my head ends up looking like the pilot's.

"I won't warn you again," says Gloria, as quiet as before, calm even as we fall towards the ground, but with an iciness in her voice that reminds me of the yellow cloud.

YELLOW AND PURPLE   85

Agent Bradden points his gun at *her*, now. "She's the cause!" he shouts, his body shaking but somehow the gun remaining steady. "It was this reject all along! There's a *reason* we were taking her back to Fressus! They sometimes *exhibit*. She's polluting us, polluting your brain, we have to kill her to prevent it! She's a dirty failure, impure, evil, should be on an animal transport, not a passenger ship. Our mission, Lefos! We're armed to terminate if there are unexpected effects. What counts, if this doesn't?" Spittle flies from his mouth as he tells her all this, as he calls me unfair names. And yet the words sound familiar, because bullies said similar things to me or Opal at some of the places we lived.

Gloria sighs. "Sorry, kid, but he's right," she says without looking at me, lowering her gun. "The mission comes first. I've always let feelings get in the way, it's why I haven't been promoted." She is presumably talking to Agent Bradden now. "I should have listened to you at the start." She steps to one side. "Apologies, Bradden."

There's a bang. And another, and another.

But it's Agent Bradden that falls back, blood coming from two holes in his chest and one in his head. His gun clatters to the ground, while he smashes against the controls then flops onto his face on the floor.

His head didn't pop like a melon, and despite what I thought earlier, I don't laugh after all.

Gloria's hand isn't shaking. She'd moved and fired in the same second he aimed at me. It was so quick and smooth I bet she's done that before, too.

She kicks Agent Bradden's gun away and then checks him but it's pretty clear, even to me, that he's dead. This isn't like a film-cast where people get shot and then say their last words before they properly die.

He doesn't have any last words.

Maybe I shouldn't have thought about film-casts. There's also the scary ones where a baddie gets killed and looks dead but *then gets up again for his revenge*! I hope Gloria checked him properly.

I'm going to make sure I watch his body for a while.

"You okay?" she asks, operating the controls fast after she slips her pistol back into her jacket.

"Yep," I answer. "I am now."

We're falling.

We're going to crash.

While Gloria reactivates systems I look up through the bubble of cockpit glass. The yellow clouds are gone, just blackness above, but even though there's no sun there are shadows on the violet world below, which I know is wrong. Details appear now, like swirls of high pinkish sand dune, and weird building shapes that rise out of it, and some circles that might be domes, or even dips in the sand that are filled with shadows. Some areas have giant line patterns etched into the rock, at a scale that would probably be invisible if viewed from the ground.

"I'm turning on the emergency AI," she says. "I've only got basic pilot qualifications, so that will do a better job of reducing the impact. Then we just need to prepare for a bumpy landing."

The fact that I can see all that detail below us is pretty bad, because it means we're *really* near the ground. Even though we're slowing all the time, and kind of gliding, the landscape rushes towards us so fast that it might be slightly worse than *bumpy*.

But I am not scared.

Gloria drags me to a passenger seat, one by the aisle, not the window, and closes the cockpit door behind us. At least we don't have to see blood and bodies. This seat is padded and impact-resistant, with no hard edges for bashing injuries. She loosens the straps, puts me on her lap, and clips us in together. She opens her legs so I'm between them, then closes them firm, and she wraps her arms around me tight, then leans over me. It's like being within a shell, and she feels strong, and sturdy, and reminds me of Opal's protectiveness, and that's all good.

"Don't worry," Gloria whispers.

"I won't. You're super tough. You got those upgraded bones and stuff."

"That's it. Think of me as a cage."

She means a protective one, like a vehicle roll cage, but it does remind me of how all this started, a cage as prisoner and bars, a cage where someone is taken away from where they want to be.

"And if I don't make it," Gloria adds, "then –"

Boom

Black, full black where no light shines through thin-skin eyelids, so there are no whooshes of red-purple, which is just blood pumping in the thin skin. If you don't see the swoosh you might not be alive.

My skull throbs like the worst headache ever, and that's only a bit worse than the aching everywhere else. My teeth feel like they've been pulled out. Maybe they clacked together so hard that they *have* fallen out.

It's still black when I open my eyes, and at first I imagine this is really being dead, and I don't like it; but then there's hissing, and the impact foam gets washed away from where it encased us, falling off in the nose-stinging gas jet, crumbling away to nothing. As it dissolves I can breathe and move, and there's a plum-coloured light. As soon as I get my arms free I unclip the belt and climb off her, brushing away the last pieces of disintegrating foam.

The back of the shuttle is all crumpled in, and a big piece of the craft's side across the aisle is ripped open, leaving a jagged tear in the hull. Through the gap is sand. Amethyst sand. And something shimmering beyond it.

I can breathe. That's good. Fresh, like a sea breeze.

I check Gloria. She's breathing too. I put my hand on her chest and do feel a heartbeat, and it's a strong one, but she doesn't wake up when I speak to her or rub her cheek or lift her (supermax heavy) hand to hold it in mine.

There should be a first aid kit somewhere. If it's advanced then it might be able to wake her up or do diagnostics. I look for one, and get distracted by something outside the rip in the shuttle's hull, so I step out through the gap in the jagged metal onto crunchy, shifting sand. The shimmery thing is a dome of about fifty metres across, which covers the shuttle and the area around us. From my position inside the dome I can see through it to the dunes beyond, and the vague shapes of what might be buildings, or squat skytowers, but mist makes the horizon indistinct. There's a faint smell to the air which I hadn't noticed at first. Maybe a kind of fishyness.

The silt beneath me moves, sort of ripples. I look down at my bare feet, hoping I won't see anything reaching up, but I just see my toes, a funny colour in the purpleness, and that gritty, scratchy surface squidges between them. No one is drawing the shapes, unless they're *underneath* the sand.

"Hello," I say. "Do you know anything about first aid? My friend needs help."

And the sand ripples some more, and this time I hear a voice in my head, and it has hints of Bobo, except a Bobo that speaks like a low-res signal picked up from far away and listened to in real time rather than waiting for it to cache together.

{One of import, finally here, glad welcome. We can attend you both.}

"I'm fine, just sore. It's Gloria I'm worried about."

{You are our possession object now, belonging, we will act what needs.}

"Erm, thanks. Where are you?" I glance around, expecting to see someone stood on the shuttle roof. The craft has dug a huge furrow into the sand, and the nose is buried in it, which means the two bodies in the cockpit are kind of buried now, especially if the glass smashed when we crashed.

{Do not worry. We have plans for you.}

It's hard when they speak, because something sort of flashes behind my eyes, so I can't even look at whatever moves under the lavender sand. "I said I'm *not* worried about me. It's my friend. Can you fix her or not?"

{Yes. We can fix.}

And something stings me.

I say "Ouch" and look down, and catch a glimpse of something disappearing under the grit, like a pointy bit of an insect, which makes me think of scorpion stingers. There's a tiny hole in my heel, and a growing drop of blood.

I am tired.

I drop to my knees in the sand. It reminds me of a fake beach on Fressus, oh so long ago. And it's unfair that we never know when something is the last time until *afterwards*: so there was a last time that I slept in my own bed, or explored that beach, and I thought it would happen again but it never did. The time's already gone. And there's worse, because the last time I saw Mummy and Daddy and Opal I didn't do a final hug or say that I loved them. We never *know*.

"What did you ...?" But my mouth is too gummy to speak.

And I can still hear them, but I don't think they're talking to me any more.

{Losing many in entry struggle against symbionts. What about the other this here? It is also altered from species forty-seven template.}

{No connection to us. Intra enhancements, not Null divergence content.}

{Source of data, possibly, more than the other grief sadness forty-sevens being dismantled. Suggestion is disassembly here, too.}

{We can research disassemble analyse both. Rebuild copy duplicates with implanteds for same result.}

{Negative agree. Propose keep both here, just analyse. Attempt stasis system again. High probability revival state. May be not fatal now.}

{May. May not. We will consult further.}

But the words are getting hazy, and my head is heavy, so I lie on the sand. It's not scratchy now, it's super soft, like the best bed. I close my eyes. It is black, but swooshy. I hope they look after us. And I remember the sand of the past, crunching under my toes as I held Opal's hand, just the two of us alone in the universe, and her telling me it wasn't my fault, and she was my sister, and she loved me. I call out to her, as if she is by my side, and I think I hear her but maybe I'm already dreaming, because she's crying and she never cries. So tired, so floaty, maybe I'll dream of Opal, maybe I'll dream of Mummy and Daddy, or Bobo will come to me. Maybe I'll wake and still be in Gloria's arms. Sleep is always another world, and sometimes you just have to accept that the universe isn't perfect or fair, and there's not much you can do about it if you're just one itty bitty person. Opal said something like that, and I'm too tired to resist the hurt and the sleepiness any more.

NIGHTMARE MAN

ABOUT THE AUTHOR

Karl Drinkwater is an author with a silly name and a thousand-mile stare. He writes dystopian space opera, dark suspense and diverse social fiction. If you want compelling stories and characters worth caring about, then you're in the right place. Welcome!

Karl lives in Scotland and owns two kilts. He has degrees in librarianship, literature and classics, but also studied astronomy and philosophy. Dolly the cat helps him finish books by sleeping on his lap so he can't leave the desk. When he isn't writing he loves music, nature, games and vegan cake.

Go to karldrinkwater.uk to view all his books grouped by genre.

As well as crafting his own fictional worlds, Karl has supported other writers for years with his creative writing workshops, editorial services, articles on writing and publishing, and mentoring of new authors. He's also judged writing competitions such as the international Bram Stoker Awards, which act as a snapshot of quality contemporary fiction.

Don't Miss Out!

Enter your email at karldrinkwater.substack.com to be notified about his new books. Fans mean a lot to him, and replies to the newsletter go straight to his inbox, where every email is read. There is also an option for paid subscribers to support his work: in exchange you receive additional posts and complimentary books.

OTHER TITLES BY KARL DRINKWATER

STANDALONE SUSPENSE
Turner
They Move Below
Harvest Festival

MANCHESTER SUMMER
Cold Fusion 2000
2000 Tunes

CONTEMPORARY SHORT STORIES
It Will Be Quick

NON-FICTION
From Idea To Item

COLLECTED EDITIONS
Karl Drinkwater's Horror Collection
Lost Solace Five Book Edition

Author's Notes

Lost Tales of Solace are side stories set in the Lost Solace universe. They are all standalone tales, but readers who are familiar with the main Lost Solace novels will gain the most from them.

In the chronology of the series, this story occurs in the UFS year 437, thirteen years before the events of the novel Lost Solace take place.

I'd always felt that Clarissa's story needed to be told, since it is so central to Opal's story. Until now, we'd only met Clarissa during a brief memory scene in Chasing Solace (which diverged from reality and morphed into a nightmare towards the end). I wanted to get into Clarissa's mind. It's why I chose to write this in the first person, finally giving her a voice.

All the plot reversals evolved from trying to create the world with Clarissa at the centre. At the start Clarissa hopes her bad-ass older sister will rescue her, but it turns out Clarissa is pretty good at rescuing herself. Likewise, the Agents are equally bad and hated by her at the start, but by the end she is friends with one. I also had fun with the transition from Clarissa's powerful internal life to her burgeoning engagement with the external world.

All the other Lost Tales so far have an AI element. Helene is mostly dialogue with an AI; Grubane is told from the perspective of an AI; Ruabon (my next novella) involves a few low-level AI helpers. But AIs weren't appropriate for Clarissa's story, where they would have felt shoehorned in. Instead I created Freddie Bobo: not an AI, but fulfilling the role of a non-human intelligence with its own motivations.

Fun fact: all the Lost Tales have interstitial chapters, where documents are gradually revealed that reflect on the plot of the story, whilst also filling in details of the world and characters. Helene had Aseides' Law Of Nuvo-Emergent AI Development; Grubane had the famous major's treatise on The Philosophy And Application Of Ancient Games. My next tale, Ruabon, will have Diagnostics Archives, illustrating the formation of each droid's secret personality. However, when writing Clarissa I went well over my word count, so couldn't add much to the interstitial chapters. Then I had the brainwave of including Clarissa's drawings, which were originally mentioned in Chasing Solace. It meant I could keep the interstitial structure of the other Lost Tales, without going further over my word limit. Genius. Thanks, Clarissa, I owe you some RearroBlox.

Thanks

Thanks as usual to my Insider Team superstars for their feedback on early drafts, particularly John-Michael, Charles, Angela, and Alyson.

Special thanks to the AI that recreated Clarissa's doodles. I sent it through time and space to retrieve them from Opal and Clarissa's Mossareid apartment just before the next set of tenants moved in. These are the only remaining sketches done by Clarissa between 434 and 437 (UFS years).

I'm grateful to Helen Pryke for her final checks of the text, spotting my errors and typos.

Many thanks to Taig (and my other Kickstarter backers) for supporting the paperback version's genesis and having such faith in my work.

Thank you for reading this book, and for supporting me and my work. If you have a moment, please review it on Goodreads or at the store where you bought it. Even a few words about what you enjoyed can encourage someone else to take a chance on a new tale. I wish you many glasses of StrawberryFizz!

www.ingramcontent.com/pod-product-compliance
Lightning Source LLC
Chambersburg PA
CBHW020425130626
46549CB00006B/2743